ST. NICHOLAS
AND THE DRAGON

A Dragonsbard Tale

By Tracy & Laura Hickman

Tracy Hickman
2012

Laura Hickman

Dedication:

To all our Grandchildren;
From Your Nanny and Papa.

Scribe's Forge Publishing
P.O. Box 1167
Riverton, Utah 84065

ISBN:
978-0-9799725-2-2

TABLE OF CONTENTS

Prologue:
Once Upon a Thyme

nce upon a Yuletide Eve, a thick snowfall swirled into the village of Eventide on a biting northern wind. It whisked down the Mordale road past Wishing Lane and over the cobblestones of Fall's Court. It whistled mournfully over the crest of the gentle Bolly Falls rushing from beneath the ice past the newly reconstructed mill on the Wanderwine River. It spun like frozen spindrift around the corner of Charter Square and took another swing at the wooden sign suspended over the heavy door. The wind did not care to read the sign which was, perhaps, the wind's loss for it proclaimed the establishment to be the Griffin's Tale Inn. If the wind had known where it was it might have stopped for a while and taken a rest, for Squire Tomas Melthalion's establishment was known throughout Windriftshire for its hospitality. It was also known as the fabled inn that survived the attack of the dragon Khrag – largely because that was the story that Squire Tomas insisted on telling everyone who came into the Inn whether they had heard the story or not. Tomas also never failed to mention that Princess Aerthea herself had taken rooms in his Inn during the funeral of Farmer Benis ... and that he had known Benis personally. But at this late hour, the wind would have not carried the Innkeeper's words with it into the night ... for the Squire had long since retired and the door to the Inn was well bolted against the gale.

On the other side of the door, the howling protest of the wind was muted and unheeded. Here was a great common room of the Inn, a very snug and cozy refuge, indeed. The low ceiling, held firmly in place by thick, dark oak beams gave the room an intimate feeling of joy from the garlands and bright fruit still festooned the hall. The inn was kept warm and inviting by the enormous fireplace that occupied the entire eastern wall of the room. But at this late hour of the night, the roar of the fire's blaze from the earlier festivities of the evening had settled quietly into a more modest, sleepy crackle. The chairs were unoccupied. The wooden tables were cleared and wiped clean.

All that remained were two men doing their best to make themselves comfortable on a pair of benches they had pulled up close to the fire.

"Truly, Abel! Is this not the most agreeable of accommodations," sighed the Dragonsbard as he rolled up his winter cape into what might pass at least the first part of the night as his pillow.

This companion and scribe believed in his heart that more accommodating accommodations would have easily been within their reach upstairs if the Dragonsbard had not lost their savings earlier in the evening in a game of King's Cards.

"Oh, you're just in a mood because that Melodi Morgan girl has not returned home from Mordale for the Yule celebration," the Bard snapped back. "Don't try and deny it! The truth is that we're in a bad fix,

Dragon's Bard Tales

Abel, and there's no putting a good face on it. I'm not called the Dragon's Bard for nothing! Unless I come up with a set of proper stories to satisfy that old dragon Khrag at the first of the New Year then he might just decide to eat me after all!"

Abel considered the tall and rather skinny Bard and wondered if there were enough meat on his bones to make it worth the trouble to eat him. Another glance at the hardwood bench convinced him to suggest imposing themselves on other lodgings for the night.

"We've been all over that," the Dragonsbard shrugged as he sat on a rumpled blanket he had spread over the bench as though the thick wool would be enough to soften and smooth out the hard polished wood beneath him. "Jarod and Caprice would have hosted us at Morgan House but my performance was extended well past proper hours for us to make the journey up Wishing Lane through the snow – and as Melodi is not returned home you would hardly be motivated to push through the drifts. Beulandreus Dudgeon offered us a room as well but the thought of staying with a dwarf below ground filled me with no small sense of dread... and before you say another word, you know very well that Mrs. Walters would not

[8]

have offered us so much as a barrel to sleep in at her husband's cooperage at any price and that the pixies are always invited over to the Oakmans for Yule's Eve and I can't abide their nonsense. It's hardly my fault that there were no rooms left in the Inn by the time our game of King's Cards ended. The Squire could hardly be expected to toss paying lodgers out into the cold."

Able was about to tell the Dragonsbard just who he thought should be tossed into the snow when a series of thumps resounded through the darkened common room. Both the bard and his scribe ducked down instinctively from the sound above their heads, a succession of muffled poundings that soon slowed and then stopped. They waited motionless for a time, anticipating perhaps the imminent collapse of the inn around them but there was no further sound than the quiet crackling of the fire.

The scribe pulled his blanket tighter around him in the deepening shadows of the large room while muttering the common sentiments so often expressed by the ladies on Cobblestone Street that perhaps they were all about to be murdered in their beds.

"But it is Yuletide Eve!" the Dragonsbard exclaimed, spreading his hands in a grand gesture that Abel always took to mean that the argument was settled without having to make sense. "What can possibly go wrong on a festive night like this?"

A frigid blast of winter rushed into the room, tossing embers from the fire into the air and mixing them with a rush of snowflakes and glittering flecks of ice. Both the Bard and his Scribe shrank from the sudden flurry, blinking against a sudden onslaught of ice, sleet and snow. Just as suddenly the chill gale subsided.

There, standing inside the still barred door, stood an enormous man.

He wore a long, fur-trimmed coat of crimson-dyed weave held closed around his considerable girth by golden toggles and a wide black sash also trimmed in gold. A long stocking cap sat firmly on his head and covered his ears. It had a fur tassel at its peak which hung down to his right and rested against his shoulder. His enormous black boots were fur-lined as well. In his large right hand he squeezed a pair of padded leather mittens which he had seemingly just removed while his left hand was gathered around the top of a large sack that he slung over his left shoulder.

But it was his face that caught their attention at once. His bulbous nose was reddened from the chill of the storm outside as were both of his round cheeks. These were made all the brighter, however, by the surrounding explosion of brilliant white beard that hung out over his coat and the long hair he had gathered at the back of his cap. There was the hint of perpetual laughter about his brilliant blue eyes which Abel liked at once and which the Bard found to be disconcerting.

"Merry Yule!" the man said in a deep voice that seemed to fill every corner of the large room even though it was spoken in hushed tones. "May a traveler sojourn with you for a brief time? I saw the fire and am in need of a short rest in my journey."

"For myself and my apprentice," the Bard said standing and cocking his head, "we are grateful for the company though, I must confess to you that we are not the proprietors of this establishment and it is not with our powers to offer you shelter for the night."

"You need not be concerned," the large man chuckled with deep amusement. "I never stay anywhere on my journeys for long."

"And," continued the Bard with his most winning smile, "in whose company do we find ourselves this night?"

"You may call me Nicholas," the man said as he stepped closer toward the sputtering fire. He laid down his sack and, pulling an armed chair from atop one of the tables, set it down by the hearth and settled his enormous size into it. That the chair accommodated his size was somewhat surprising.

"And I," said the Bard with as much dramatic flair as he could muster at this late hour, "Am the *Dragonsbard!* No doubt you have heard of me in your..."

"Yes, Edvard, I know who you are, who you were and who you think you may yet be ... and you as well, Master Abel." The large man waved his hand still clutching his gloves in faint dismissal. He sighed and leaned back, stretching his legs and wiggling his feet. He closed his eyes and asked. "Have you passed the thyme yet?"

"Well," the Bard replied. "We were playing cards earlier, which I suppose counts as passing the time."

"No, Edvard, not <u>time</u> ... I mean thyme," the large man with the great beard corrected softly as he leaned forward in his chair. He removed his cap and the snow-white hair seemed to shine in the faint light of the dying fire. "In the ancient days, thyme was a symbol of strength and courage. When I was a boy, we passed around a sprig of thyme on Yule's Eve in as a reminder of an old story and wonderful story – probably forgotten now – from those days... Oh! That reminds me, I believe I have something for you Master Abel!"

"Wait!" the Bard asked quickly with considerable insistence in his voice. "What do you mean about a forgotten story."

"Patience, Edvard!" the old man laughed and the sound of it was like bright bells. He continued to rummage through his sack and at last produced a small box wrapped in cloth and tied with a bright ribbon.

Abel took the box with a quizzical smile.

"I believe it is past midnight." The man's white beard quivered as he chuckled. "You may open it now if you like but I would be careful with the wrappings – one never knows when they may come in useful."

The bard was insistent. "But this story, you say it is forgotten..."

"It is not your turn," Nicholas insisted, his eyes intent on Abel as the scribe pulled open the lid on the box.

Abel's eyebrows fell from excitement into deep puzzlement.

"Well, let us see," urged Nicholas.

Abel pulled a small broach from the box. It was a thin lattice of silver worked into an intricate and delicate pattern that resembled a rose. The piece would have been impressive and lovely on a woman ... and exactly the kind of thing that would be completely useless as part of Abel's meager wardrobe.

Still, the confused scribe thanked the old gentleman for his bizarre gift.

The Bard tried his best to steer the conversation back to something that involved him. "But about this story..."

"Edvard the Just," Nicholas' voice boomed. The old man had released his belt and undone the toggles on his coat, allowing his large stomach the freedom to bounce under his linen shirt as he laughed. He stroked his beard, thinking as he spoke. "You were always impatient. Even as a boy you could never sit still through the epic tales. It seems there is nothing more difficult for a storyteller to do than to listen to someone else's tale. But the truth is that I've brought you a gift as well tonight and, if you'll have a little patience, I'll give it to you after my story is done. Agreed?"

"Most heartily," the Bard nodded, thinking that perhaps he had found the story that would keep him from becoming the dragon Khrag's next meal.

"This is a story about the court of old Wenceslas..."

"King Wenceslas?" the Bard offered.

"He was never a king, he was a Duke," Nicholas replied, his bright eyes narrowing. "And it may not have been that Wenceslas after all. I get so confused sometimes as to the where and the when that I am. And it involves me, too, though I was much younger then. It's about a knight on a quest one Yule's Eve like tonight and how the tradition of thyme got started."

"And you played a part in this story?" the Bard asked.

"I did," Nicholas nodded as he leaned forward in his chair.

"What did you do?"

"I brought the head of a dragon back to the court of Wenceslas," Nicholas breathed quietly over the crackle of the fire. "And if you'll quit interrupting me, I'll tell you how."

Chapter 1:
The Problem with Dragons

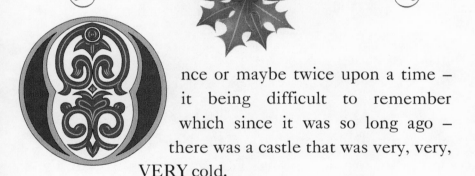

nce or maybe twice upon a time –
it being difficult to remember
which since it was so long ago –
there was a castle that was very, very,
VERY cold.

It was also true that the castle was very OLD, but
that fact was not what concerned Duke Wenceslas, the
ruler of the Duchy of Grand Wences, as he sat
shivering on his throne. It was the cold in the Great
Hall of his keep not its age that kept his teeth
chattering and caused his crown to shake on his head.

Duke Wenceslas looked mournfully over at the enormous hearth to one side of the hall. It was almost twenty feet across and ten feet tall in the center. The plinth base was polished granite. The legs and header around the firebox had been carved with a procession of the Duke's ancestors, lords, knights, and peasants who had come to claim the duchy uncounted years before. The mantle was festooned with bows for the Yuletide while the overmantle and crown framed a wonderful tapestry of the Duke and the Duchess Wenceslas.

Yet there was no cheery blaze within its carved stone maw of its firebox. No warm radiance filling the hall. No dancing light from its flickering flames. The fireplace was as cold as the room before it.

In the Duke's hands he held a bundle of thyme. He traditionally awarded it each Yuletide Eve to the bravest of his champions. Tonight he was wondering, as he stared at the hearth, how well it might burn.

Before Wenceslas in the enormous room stood all the gathered courtiers, summoned at his command. They were as miserable as the Duke. The knights rattled in their armor. The squires squirmed in their hose and doublets. The ladies trembled in their long gowns and thick wraps.

You might suspect that St. Nicholas was in the hall shivering as well – although he was not yet considered a saint at the time – but you would be wrong. Nicholas is not yet to be found either in the hall or our story here as yet.

Who were in the hall, however, were Lord Erok and Lord Ayhard – the two freeholders of farmland in the Duchy – stood in their long, heavy coats before the Duke, each of them speaking with heated eloquence though their words did nothing to warm the room or the Duke's disposition.

"...And I'm sure that Your Grace will readily acknowledge that it is the duty of his royal personage to address our grievances at once!" Lord Erok had worked himself up to a frenzy of speech which made him rather proud of himself but did little to endear him anyone else in the room. "Too long we have waited..."

"Far too long!" piped up Lord Ayhard who rarely got a word in between Erok's long winded words without either taking advantage of Erok catching his breath or, barring that, the calculated wedging of words in those spaces where Erok actually tried to think rather than speak.

"Far, FAR too long," Erok shouted in continuance, his words billowing out in puffs of breath that hung as icy clouds between him and the frowning Wenceslas. "We have waited for the crown to do SOMETHING to safeguard the lives of the peasants and the serfs working our land and more importantly our CATTLE!"

"And our SHEEP!" Lord Ayhard wedged in, insuring that his own holdings were represented in the grievance as it was presented.

The increasing order of precedence given by Lord Erok and his neighbor Lord Ayhard was, as everyone in the hall knew, entirely intentional.

"And now what is the result?" Lord Erok exclaimed. Frost from his own breath was starting to encrust his beard in the chilly hall. "Our peasants cannot even enter the forest and harvest wood for our fires to keep us warm through this dreadful winter! The axes are silent as the falling snow, the stores of firewood are utterly depleted. There is not a stick left of any table, bed, chair or stool to be found among the peasant cottages for their being burned in the hearths."

"My Lords," Duke Wenceslas raised his hand as though trying to deflect the frosty words of Erok and Ayhard. "It is truly a terrible hardship on the peasants..."

"Aye! But worse still," Erok shouted, "what about Yuletide?"

"Yuletide?" Wenceslas squinted. The Duke was wondering if the chill had somehow effected his hearing. "What of Yuletide?"

"The feast, My Lord!" Erok responded.

"Yes, I understand what the Yuletide Feast is," the Duke snapped. "What does that have to do with..."

"He means, sire, however shall we hold the Great Feast if we cannot even build a fire to cook it?" Lord Ayhard sputtered as though he were stating the obvious.

Duke Wenceslas shook though it may not have been from the cold. "The peasants are freezing, burning their furniture to keep warm and you're worried about your revelry?"

"It's a tradition!" Lord Erok asserted, puffing up his chest.

"A FINE tradition!" Lord Ayhard affirmed, trying to puff his own chest out further than his neighbor.

"And a tradition that I believe can be saved!" Lord Erok affirmed. From within the folds of his coat, the freeholder produced a large scroll of velum. Erok approached the throne and, kneeling, presented the scroll to Duke Wenceslas.

The Duke groaned, laying the bundle of thyme in his lap as he reached out and took the scroll. His gloved hands fumbled with it for a moment before he managed to open the unusually long document. The illuminations were very pretty but the writing was also so small that even the Duke (whose sight was actually quite good) was having trouble reading it.

"And what is this, Lord Erok?" the Duke asked.

"It is a decree, My Lord," Erok replied.

"A ROYAL decree," Ayhard added.

The rest of the courtiers in the room groaned.

"Again?" the Duke asked though his eyes never left the velum scroll.

"Yes, Your Grace!" Lord Erok nodded. "It creates, by your will, and appoints an emergency commission tasked with the procurement and distribution of all types of wood within the borders of your kingdom. It grants to this commission emergency powers over the knights, militia, bowmen, men-at-arms, and guards and extends the provision to the labor procurement of serfs and peasants...

"As well as essential services such as axe makers, sharpeners, smithies and miners," Lord Ayhard added.

"And thereby addresses this imminent threat to our Yuletide celebrations," Lord Erok concluded.

The Duke looked up over the top edge of the scroll. Frost coated his thick and normally dark eyebrows so heavily that his scowl was somewhat softened. "And just who, I fear to ask, do you suggest to head this emergency commission?"

"We believe that freeholders should head such a council," Lord Erok said without batting a frozen eyelash. "Men who know how distribution of goods may best be administered for the betterment of the kingdom."

"And the preservation of our Yuletide Feast," Lord Ayhard piped in.

""We shall put an end to any slackness on the part of your subjects and get the job done," Lord Erok concluded with a slight bow.

Duke Wenceslas turned to the throne next to his. The Duchess Wenceslas was the most beautiful woman the Duke had ever beheld although it was difficult now to behold her very well, wrapped as she was in so many layers of ermine robes, wraps and blankets. Still, her sweet, narrow face peeking out from above the shawl and below the cowl was frowning. Her blue eyes were bright and disbelieving.

"The problem is not our subjects," the Duchess insisted. "Certainly not with the peasants."

"No, it is not," Duke Wenceslas agreed. "The problem is the dragon."

Lord Erok stammered. "But this commission, Your Grace..."

"Why do the axmen not go into the woods?" Duke Wenceslas asked without waiting for an answer. "It's because of the dragon! Every time they enter the forest, the dragon attacks them, driving them back to their villages!"

"Yes, My Lord," Lord Ayhard nodded his head. "But if you'll look under section fifteen, subsection thirty-two, paragraph five of the commission's mandate..."

"I've read it," Duke Wenceslas replied, casting the scroll down at the feet of Lord Erok and Lord Ayhard. "It gives the commission authority to muster the knights to defend <u>your</u> cattle, Lord Erok and <u>your</u> sheep, Lord Ayhard, from the incessant abduction of your stock by the dragon!"

"Our livestock," Lord Erok snarled as he snatched up the scroll from the frosty stone floor at his feet, "are strategic national resources!"

"And essential to the Yuletide Eve Celebrations!" squeaked Lord Ayhard.

"And our knights have been out guarding your cattle and your sheep," Wenceslas countered, "and has this gotten anyone a single stick of wood?"

"Well, not as yet, Your Grace," Lord Erok replied.

"What is the cause of our problems? It is the dragon!" Duke Wenceslas said forcefully as he rose to stand before his throne, grasping the bundle of thyme in his hand as though it were a sword. "Who keeps us from harvesting the bountiful woods of our duchy? The dragon! Who is it that takes the cattle and the sheep from your fields, my Lords? The dragon! My people are freezing and starving and what is the cause? The dragon! I hardly need a commission of Lords to tell me where my duty lies in this matter!"

"But, Your Grace!" Lord Erok said. "The entire point of this commission..."

"Sir George!" Duke Wenceslas called out into the hall, his own breath condensed and drifting into the frigid air. "Sir George!"

From among the knights in their clattering armor stepped a single warrior. His own armor was quite different from the rest. It shone brilliantly even in the dim light of the frozen hall, polished to perfection. A great red plume swept backward from the crest of the helmet which the knight held firmly in the crook of his left arm. His face was carefully shaved, exposing the dimple of his strong chin. His chiseled features were beautifully framed by long locks of curly hair.

"My liege," said Sir George with a rakish look. "I am here, sire!"

"Are you the greatest knight in all the land?" Duke Wenceslas demanded.

"Why, yes, my liege," Sir George agreed, smiling with a wink as he tossed his curls slightly in affirmation.

"Then tonight you will go out and slay this dragon!" Duke Wenceslas commanded.

Sir George blinked. His radiant smile dimmed slightly but his eyes were fixed to the bundle of thyme in the Duke's hands. It was an honor he had hoped to win that night. "I beg your pardon, My Lord?"

"You will go out to the fields on the other side of the village where Lord Erok keeps his cattle," Duke Wenceslas went on. "We will withdraw the knights from their guard duty and when the dragon comes to take the cattle you will slay it."

"Of course, my liege," said Sir George, holding up a polished, steel-clad finger on his right hand. "But, Your Grace, tonight might not be the best night for dragon-slaying. The conditions require..."

"You will go out into the far fields," Duke Wenceslas demanded, "you will slay this dragon and you will bring his head to me here in the hall tonight! If you were looking for a gift to give to me this Yuletide then this is what I ask!"

"Yes, my liege!" Sir George nodded, and bit his lower lip even as he smiled.

"Tonight!" Duke Wenceslas demanded. "The dragon's head in my hall tonight!"

Chapter 2:
The Problem with Humans

t the very same once or maybe twice upon a time – it being the same once or twice upon a time as was taking place in the freezing hall of Duke Wenceslas – there was to the west an enormous cavern deep beneath the towering and snow-capped mountains that was very, very, VERY warm.

It was also true that this cavern was far older than any castle built on the verge of the eastern steppes but that fact was not the concern of Quarg, King of the

Dragons as he roasted miserably on his stone throne lit by the lava-filled crags all around him.

Quarg looked with exhausted frustration at the fissures breaking the ground all around his throne. He had chosen this cavern for its rather dramatic lighting – the red illumination coming up from the jagged gaps in the floor of the cavern gave an impression of power and has a slimming effect which minimized his growing paunch. Better still, it was an excellent place for him to cook his feasts.

He was not alone in his misery. For contrary to the belief of the humans freezing in their hall not twenty leagues to the east, there was not one but an entire court of dragons who lived under the Western Mountains all of whom had been called to council in Quarg's increasingly uncomfortable cave. Arbadeth, the blue dragon, lay back against one wall, fanning herself to no avail with her left wing. Embrag, the green dragon, lay flat against the stones hoping somehow they would cool him. Obrecht, the white dragon of the north, tried desperately to stay awake in the heat, his enormous head lolling back from time to time and striking a stalactite hanging down from the ceiling, the bump jarring him back to startled consciousness. All told there were more than a dozen dragons who had come to the hall and all of them despondent over the heat in the underground grotto.

Now you might expect St. Nicholas to be standing in the midst of the dragons, bravely facing these winged monsters – but still you would be wrong. That comes later. For now, Nicholas is nowhere near being a saint but he does come into the story very soon, indeed.

It was, instead, a rather stunning looking silver dragon by the name of Perak that bowed before Quarg panting slightly from the warmth that permeated the cavern.

"Are you trying to make a fool of this court?" King Quarg snarled, shifting uncomfortably on his hot stone throne.

"No, King Quarg!" Perak protested. "Your order was that I discover why the monstrous humans were angry with us."

"But ... but this story of yours is just too unbelievable!" Quarg complained.

"It is nevertheless true, great king!" Perak panted in the heat. Talking seemed to be making him warmer. "The humans of the plains are under the delusion that the cows and the sheep somehow belong to them alone and will attack any decent dragon who tries to harvest one."

"So they are hunting us because we are hunting cows?" Quarg shook his great, horned head, trying to comprehend such thoughts.

"Incredible as it may sound," Perak nodded. "The humans think they OWN the cows ... and the sheep as though they were some sort of 'living treasure'. This is why they have bred a type of human they call a 'knight'..."

"Ah! Now we get to the real monster!" King Quarg said, lifting up the claw of his right forepaw as comprehension dawned on him. "You mean that metal-skinned human with the sharp, hard claws."

"They're called swords, your majesty," Perak corrected. "Or spears, pikes or maybe halberds..."

"Whatever..." Quarg replied dismissively. "The point is that if the humans are claiming the cows and the sheep, when will it all stop? We've had to keep the humans out of the forests or they would even claim those animals as well. As it is, the game in the forest has gotten scarce ... the Midwinter's Feast is tomorrow and we have no cows to roast for the celebration!"

"Nor are we likely to have any, I fear," Perak sighed. "This ferocious 'knight' will most likely be guarding the cows tonight still."

"But, it's Midwinter's Feast!" Quarg sputtered. "How can we have a feast without a cows to roast?

Now, it must be admitted that humans really know very little about dragons. After all, how much can a human being really learn between the first moment a dragon appears flying over the edge of your field and the next moment when you're running away screaming? This has led to a considerable misunderstanding by humans about the nature of dragonkind.

The first fact that might surprise humans who were not so busy fleeing in panic might be that dragons are wonderful cooks. They have a tremendous and innate talent for the culinary arts although their practical skills are largely limited to roasting. They do not gobble up cows, sheep, elk, deer or any number of different fish whole and raw but take them back to their lairs where they very carefully prepare the meat and cook it. Indeed, it was one of the reasons that Quarg originally selected this particular cavern since it would afford him the opportunity to cook his meals properly over the exposed lava pits in the crags around him and afford him the opportunity to cook a great deal of meat at the same time for his Midwinter Feast guests.

The second is the unspoken and deep seated fact that humans frighten dragons more than any other creatures. While humans are small and appear to be easy prey, they are smart and have mastered so many tools that dragons never know what tricky device, weapon or gizmo they may have invented with which they might surprise a dragon. Only the very bravest of dragons would even consider confronting a human.

And the idea of eating humans is utterly abhorrent to dragons. It is simply beyond their refined gourmand tastes. Indeed, if there is anything that dragons admire about humans it is their cooking skills. They often seem to have access to herbs and spices from distant lands which dragons have great difficulty in obtaining. Indeed, if a dragon were to be so mad as to attack a human at all, it is probably because he has been driven insane by the alluring smell of paprika or sage in their possession. Humans seem to have mastered some alchemy called 'baking'. This they consider a form of 'human magic' since this skill is one has largely eluded dragonkind. This may in part be due to their failed experiments in creating a proper brick oven. It may also be due to the inherent difficulty of creatures that live over a thousand years breathing fire that can melt rock in keeping track of measurement periods so small as forty-five minutes at a three-hundred and fifty degree. Mostly, however, it may be due to the fact that dragons get so excited over the prospect of baked goods that they tend to jump up and down – with catastrophic consequences to their attempted cakes and breads.

But of all the strange notions of fearsome humanity, the idea of owning food to the exclusion of others was completely beyond their experience. Cattle in a pen, sheep in a fenced field or deer running freely through the woodlands were all same to the dragons ... and keeping the dragons from providing for themselves seemed exceedingly cruel and monstrous to the dragons – even for humans.

Which was why King Quarg had sent Perak on a quest to discover more about this monstrous creature called a knight – of which he devoutly hope there was only one.

"This knight is a fearsome, terrible monster," Perak said, his voice lowered so as not to frighten the younger dragons in the hall. "They named him after 'night' which is the time when the sun's light has vanished from the sky and this most likely refers to the darkness of the knight's heart.

Several of the female dragons in the hall gasped in fear.

"He has skin of metal scales," Perak continued, with sideways glances, his voice quieter than before, "and tools of death and destruction with which to attack any poor dragon which strays into their path."

Several of the male dragons shivered in fear despite the moist, oppressive heat in the chamber.

"And it is said to be so hideous in appearance that this creature hides its single, fearsome eye behind the lowered mask of its helmet," Perak swallowed. "An eye which can paralyze a dragon with a single glance!"

Several of the female dragons in the hall swayed and thunderously fainted at the thought.

"Well, this is absolutely intolerable!" King Quarg thundered, his voice shaking the walls of the cavern and threatening to bring down several of the stalactites down on his own head. "So here is it, the eve of the Midwinter Feast and we have no cow! Have any of you flown over the forest? Perhaps one of them has strayed from the snare of these monstrous humans and migrated into the woods! That would solve our problem for the feast..."

"The problem is not going to be solved by migrating cows," came a rumbling voice from the side of the hall. "The problem is with the humans."

Doramangir was an ancient gray dragon ... older than even he could remember. He was the great magician dragon, the keeper of flight and all the magic on which dragons depend for their wondrous abilities. It was not his magic alone, however, that the dragons all revered; for his was a sage old dragon, indeed.

"Speak wisdom, Doramangir," King Quarg said, keeping his temper in check.

"The problem is with the humans and this knight monstrosity they have created," Doramangir said as he uncurled himself from around a stalagmite whose cooler surface was keeping him comfortable in the overheated cavern. "Who is it that keeps us from harvesting the cows and sheep? It is this knight! Who has kept us from flying freely through the winter sky so that we might cool our scales under the stars? None but this fearsome knight! We have thus far not seen this creature in the forest and we have managed to frighten the lesser humans from the woods and this policy alone has kept the dear and the elk safe from also being ensnared by these humans ... but when this knight comes to the forest and we know he shall, then where shall we feed then? Beyond the Midwinter's Feast, King Quarg ... where shall we harvest meat for our cooking then?"

"The problem is this knight!" decreed King Quarg. "And for dragons everywhere, his head must be brought to me here before my throne!"

The dragons in the hall glanced wide-eyed at once another. Several of the female dragons threatened to faint yet again. It was their only defense.

"Great Quarg," Perak trembled as he spoke. "Who will do this fearsome deed?"

"I need a champion!" King Quarg demanded. "Who among you will go forth to battle against this 'knight' and bring his head to me – preferably with the metal plate closed over his hideous face and deadly paralyzing eye. I need a volunteer! Anyone?"

Arbadeth slid inconspicuously down the wall and out of site. Embrag lay as flat against the stones as possible. Obrecht hid behind several stalagmites. One by one, each of the dragons became as inconspicuous as a dragon can be. Even Perak, in his shining scales, took several slow steps back from Quarg's throne.

"Anybody?" Quarg called out again. "Anyone willing to become the hero of the Midwinter's Feast by facing the knight in combat?"

"What about Vronk?" Doramangir suggested.

"Vronk?" King Quarg's eyes narrowed. "You must be joking!"

It is true that dragons are quite fond of jokes but Doramangir was not trying to be humorous. "He is a good dragon, is very clever and he has not yet gone out and done his Naming Quest. This would be a fine opportunity for him to demonstrate his bravery before all the dragon clans."

King Quarg considered for a moment, nodded and then called out. "Vronk! Step forward!"

The dragons in the great cavern all moved aside.

Slowly, perhaps more slowly than was necessary, a little dragon barely into his scales moved toward the throne of King Quarg. He was about half the size of the adult dragons in the hall. His scales were going to be a lovely golden color when he was fully grown but now in his youth they were more of a yellow-green hue. His horns were sharp but small and his claws had been blunted by his unfortunate habit of gnawing at them when he was nervous – as he was doing right now. His wings were too small for his body and his emerald eyes rather larger than usual with fear.

"Vronk," King Quarg said in a suddenly conversational and endearing tone that was the hallmark of his political acumen. It takes considerable skill as a politician to remain the king of the dragons. "So, how are you tonight, Vronk?"

Vronk looked up at the King of Dragons that was smiling down on him with his rows of long, sharp teeth. "Fine – I guess."

"You know, I've always liked you, Vronk," King Quarg said, laying his large right forepaw on the young dragon's shoulder. "I've always thought it a terrible shame that you have not had an opportunity to prove your valor to the dragons of the clan and earn your name."

Dragons are all given a name at birth that is their 'youth name' – the name that they are raised with and referred to when they are still growing up. It is not until they prove that they are an adult by succeeding on their 'Naming Quest' that they 'earn their name' and thereby become fully accepted as adults into the dragon clans.

"Oh, that's ok," Vronk mumbled, looking down at the ground.

"You're, what, five or six hundred years old now?" Quarg urged.

"I'm six," Vronk answered, still looking down at his own large dragon feet.

"Well, Vronk, today is your lucky day," King Quarg beamed. "Tonight you're going on your Name Quest on this most special Midwinter's Eve and you're going to <u>earn</u> your name! Isn't that grand?"

"Yes, King Quarg," Vronk stammered, wringing his forepaws together and wishing he could gnaw on his claws.

"And all you have to do," King Quarg said, "is bring me the head of the knight!"

Chapter 3:
The Problem in Betwixt

A s Duke Wenceslas was asking for the head of a dragon and King Quarg was asking for the head of a knight a third once or twice upon a time was taking place. But this once or twice upon a time was not happening in the castle which was a short distance to the east nor was it happening in the forest or mountains somewhat further to the west. It was not happening in the fenced and snow-covered pastures of Lord Erok to the north or the fenced and snow covered dales of Lord Ayhard to the south.

This once or twice upon a time was happening in Betwixt.

To be more exact, it was happening in the Mary Krispnes Inn where many of the townspeople had gathered on Yuletide Eve to complain about living their lives between Erok's and Ayhard's place.

Now, if you have ever been in Betwixt, you know what a difficult life it can be for those who live there. While the dragons were complaining about the lack of food and the Duke was complaining about the lack of heat and the Squires were complaining about their lack of position and poor commerce – the townsfolk in Betwixt were complaining about all of the above and more. They had suffered on meager food and little heat and under the price manipulation of the squires before but now the winter pudding of discontent was boiling over.

The cause of this sudden outrage was the lack of Yuletide fruit cake.

You might expect that Nicholas would be standing before the angry, shouting multitude, with his hands raised in an effort to help the people in Betwixt calm down and embrace a more joyful and happy Yuletide cheer – and at last you would be RIGHT. For Nicholas was, indeed, trying to get the attention of the worked-up townspeople.

"Please, no more shouting!" Nicholas called in his booming voice over the heads of the crowd. "And you'd better not cry or pout either!"

"Are you gonna tell us why?" called a man from the back.

"That's why I came to town," Nicholas answered, his cheeks red with frustration. "I'm serious now! I'll be making a list of you lot who are shouting and you'll be last for the fruitcake, I mean that now!"

Reluctantly, the crowd's yelling subsided.

"That's better!" Nicholas said, tugging down the edges of his crimson-colored brocade doublet. He thought about removing his long winter coat as the formerly freezing great room of the inn was getting considerably warm despite the absence of a fire in the hearth. "Now, what's the problem?"

"What's the problem?!" yelled Bill Frist, the local butcher.

Nicholas lowered his bushy eyebrows, directing an accusing gaze at Bill.

The butcher squirmed uncomfortably but answered in a more polite tone. "I mean, we all know the problem ... don't we?"

Nicolas sighed. He was not yet a saint in those days and his patience was being sorely tested. He was young, too: so young in fact that he could not yet even grow a beard let alone one that was white as the snow that had blanketed all of the Duchy of Wenceslas and especially the buried the town of Betwixt. The hair on his head was actually coal black in his youth. His eyes were a brilliant blue that seemed to see everything. And his hands were powerful, for Nicholas was a craftsman who fashioned all manner of wonderful materials. Wood, metal or stone were all at his command, skills he used as it pleased him best: to make presents and toys for the children of Betwixt and as many other villages as he could reach during Yuletide in his sleigh. He did not yet have a round belly to shake but even then he was slightly overweight – most people in Betwixt attributed that to his love of baked goods especially during Yuletide. Indeed, not a single person among the people of Betwixt could fault Nicholas for adding a few extra pounds during the holidays, considering the magnificent fruitcakes created by his own hand.

You may have had some experience with fruitcake in your travels and perhaps it was not a pleasant one for many have been the bakers who have tried to steal from Nicholas his recipe for Yuletide Fruitcake. This has, you should know, been the cause of much maligning of the reputation of fruitcake in general down through the many Yuletide seasons. But the true fruitcakes – the small loaves made by the skilled hands of Nicholas himself – were a delight whose loss was too bitter to contemplate.

Which, it seemed, was the cause of revolution in the Inn that night.

"I understand your concerns and your grievances," Nicholas said with sincere empathy for the assembled townsfolk, "but this isn't going to solve the problem right here and right now in Betwixt."

"It's Yuletide Eve," sniffed Two-ton Tim. He was a huge man with arms twice the size of any other man in the room. He looked like he was going to cry. "I've been thinking about having me fruitcake since harvest time."

"I know, Tim," Nicholas sighed. There was nothing that made Nicholas sadder than disappointing someone on Yuletide Eve. "I've laid up the stores to bake them, dried fruits and all – but there just isn't any way for us to bake them. The ovens are stone-cold and, as you all know, there's nothing left in Betwixt to burn."

It was true. The tables that once stood in the inn's large common room were no longer there. The benches were gone and with them the chairs. There was not a scrap of wood remaining anywhere. And that was true all over town. The supplies of winter fuel were gone. The townsfolk were sleeping on the ground in their homes. Every piece of furniture had been consumed to keep people fed and warm. There was not a stick to be found in all the town. And now the ovens were cold on the most important feast day of the year.

"It's the Duke's fault!" shouted Rupert. He was a young man who had been instructed at a university and was, therefore, filled with dangerous and radical ideas. He raised his fist into the air. "We'll burn down the castle! Down with the Duke! Who's with me?"

No one moved or answered his plea.

"How is burning down the castle going to get my fruitcakes cooked?" Nicholas asked with more gentleness than he honestly felt.

"We will have justice!" Rupert asserted.

"Yes, but you still won't have fruitcake," Nicholas replied.

"The problem isn't the Duke," Mary Krispnes said in her clear, high voice. "He's just as cold as we are … colder, I'm thinking as there be more of us here than in his court. The problem is we can't get any wood from the forest. It's them dragons that's done it."

"Down with the dragons!" Rupert shouted suddenly. "Rise up, men and women of Betwixt and break the chains of the oppressive dragons! We'll burn them out of their forests and…"

A number of men from Betwixt demanded that Rupert pipe down.

"And why do you suppose the dragons do not allow us to chop wood from the forest?" Nicholas asked.

"It's the oppression of the working class!" Rupert answered at once.

"It was a rhetorical question," Nicholas grumbled. "Is there nothing we could burn to get my fruitcakes made?"

A thoughtful silence descended on the packed room.

"Hey, aint your toys made out of wood?" asked old man Winters. He was from the counting house and considered entirely too practical for anyone's good. "We could get them out of the sleigh, break 'em up and..."

"Down with toys!" Rupert shouted. "Down with the crass commercialism of Yuletide by the..."

"We are NOT burning the children's toys just so you can have fruitcake," Nicholas thundered.

Someone stuffed an apple in Rupert's mouth.

"Then what do we do?" asked Nell, the pretty apprentice inn keeper to Mary.

Nicholas considered for a moment. Then he turned toward the innkeeper. "Mary, is this everyone in the town?"

"It better be!" Mary answered with a sniff. 'There's no more room in my Inn!"

"Right, then," Nicholas said. "It seems to me that the best thing to do would be..."

"Hail, peasants! Fear not, common folk, for I am come!" At that moment, a rough voice shouted over the heads of the assembly interrupting Nicholas. A clanking sound like pots banging together was coming through the door. The packed crowd somehow managed to squeeze out of the way. "Know that none other than Sir George, knight protector of the realm now walks among you!"

A knight, clad in his brilliant armor made his way through the crowd and all the way to the stone bar – which had replaced the wooden one some months earlier. Sir George's curly locks were drenched in sweat from his ride from Castle Wenceslas through the deepening snows. The plume sagged considerably as he gripped the edge of his helmet in his right hand. His head was held high and proud but his knees shook his armor with a rattling sound. He turned to face the packed room.

"Our good Duke Wenceslas looked out on this beastly season and decreed that the dragon shall be slain! He has appointed ME" – and Sir George's voice squeaked on the word – "to challenge the dragon in single combat, in a duel to the de... A duel to the de... I mean to say a duel to the de..."

"Death?" Mary Krispnes urged.

"Yes, precisely!" Sir George nodded.

Nicholas pushed his way through the crowd as well, coming to stand next to the knight. "So you're going to solve our problems, sir knight, by slaying this dragon on Yuletide Eve?"

"Aye!" The knight bellowed in a voice that sounded with exaggerated confidence. "I am Sir George the Dragonslayer! I have come to slay the dragon – it's what dragonslayers are supposed to do – and regain the forest in the name of the Duke and all you little people. I am to prove myself by bringing his head before the Duke in court."

"Indeed?" Nicholas asked in astonishment. "How?"

Sir George blinked at Nicholas. "I beg your pardon, boy!"

"Why, I'll just ... with my weapons, of course!" Sir George replied as the thought came to him. "I've a wagon full of all sorts of weapons donated by every other knight in the castle, only..."

The knight's voice trailed off.

"Only?"

"You see, due to the generosity of all the other knights to the cause, the wagon appears to be over-burdened."

"It's stuck in the snow, you mean."

"Yes, exactly," Sir George nodded with thanks. "No fault of my own, of course! So, I guess this means that the actual slaying of the dragon will have to be postponed until the wagon can be freed from the drifted snow bank. And I had so hoped to engage the dragon in combat tonight. We expect the beast will raid either Lord Erok's or Lord Ayhard's herds tonight but, alas, without transportation..."

"But I have a sleigh," Nicholas offered.

Sir George looked sideways at the young man in the crimson colored long coat. "You what?"

"I have a sleigh," Nicholas repeated, "and it would be my honor to accompany such a noble knight to his destiny."

"It would?" Sir George murmured.

Nicholas looked into the dark eyes of Sir George. His pupils were dancing back and forth. Sweat was beading on his brow. Nicholas was always an excellent judge of character from naughty to nice and everything in between. What he found out from looking into the eyes of Sir George was something not even Nicholas had expected.

The Knight was terrified.

"Have you ever slain a dragon before?" Nicholas asked.

"Well, what most uneducated people do not understand," Sir George said, looking up with sudden interest at the ceiling, "is that there just aren't enough dragons to go around. It's rare that a knight actually has the opportunity to engage a dragon in combat and so much of the training for dragon-slaying must be conducted on a more theoretical than practical level..."

Mary Krispnes put her fists to her hips in indignation. "You mean you've only ever slain pretend dragons?"

"I can assure you, madam," Sir George responded with rising indignation, "that our training is more thorough than is required by the actual combat!"

"But I used to gather wood in them woods," Two-ton Tim said to the knight. "I've seem that there dragon and he breathed fire down from the sky!"

"Fire?" Sir George asked, a quiver in his voice. "From the sky?"

"Aye!" Two-ton Tim affirmed. "I seen it blast the ice of a frozen lake into steam in the time it takes to snap your fingers! Consumed my cart, it did with a blaze so hot it melted the steel rims of my wheels and the bolts holding it together!"

Sir George's fingers fluttered over his breastplate, his voice suddenly quiet. "Melted ... steel?"

"Right, that," agreed Bill Frist, "that is unless the dragon prefers his meat on the rare side. Then he'll have to pry you out of that armor first either with his razor-like claws or his long, sharp teeth.

Nicholas managed to catch the knight before he fell in a metallic heap on the floor of the Inn, propping him up against the bar.

"I'm all right. No need to fuss, miss. I'm all right," Sir George mumbled as he regained consciousness.

"A dragon is coming?" Bill Frist squeaked, his voice a full octave higher than usual. "He'll burn down the village! And this is the champion the Duke has sent to stop him? That's government help for ye! Well, I say thanks anyway but it seems like we need our own champion if we're gonna save everyone in Betwixt! Does anyone even know HOW to slay a dragon?"

"I do," Nicholas said at once.

Everyone packing the Inn that night gasped at once.

"I will be your champion," Nicholas said to the people in the Inn. "I know just how to take care of this dragon."

"You mean YOU'RE going out there?" breathed Mary Krispnes.

"Well, that's the end of the fruitcake," scoffed old man Winters.

"Here, great sir knight, I'll take you off to glory and even chronicle your fatal – I mean fateful -- deeds in this epic and potentially tragic battle if you like," Nicholas grunted as he helped the knight, who was still rather weak in the knees, stagger back toward the door and out of the Inn. "And if you're as good at dragon-slaying as I think you'll be tonight, you might even get one of my fruitcakes."

Nicholas pushed the knight up into his sleigh then climbed in after him. He gave a whistle to his pair of reindeer in harness and the sleigh bound forward across the snow covered streets of Betwixt. Everyone in the Inn heard Nicholas exclaim as he drove out of sight, "Mix the cake batter now, we'll bake after the fight!"

Chapter 4: Between Eroks & Ayhard's Place

The epic battle of Sir George and Vronk took place, so royal historian's tell us, on the old Forest Road that meandered between Lord Erok's cattle fields on the north and Lord Ayhard's sheep fields on the south. Whether it actually took place ON the road is a matter of considerable speculation. The snow which had fallen so heavily earlier in the week, now lay round about not only crisp and even across the landscape but also rather deep. As the dragon had scared off anyone who would make their way back and forth from the woods, the road had remained unused and, therefore, was buried beneath a mantle of white that made it indistinguishable from the land on either side of it. The tree line of the Forest of Wenceslas lay but only half a league to the west of the site and the town of Betwixt only a league to the east. Nor were there fences by which could be gauged either side of the road. Lord Erok and Lord Ayhard had agreed between them that as long as Erok did not raise sheep and Lord Ayhard did not raise cattle there would be no confusion as to their property and the expense of fences would not be required. Therefore, the field of combat was devoid of any unnatural obstruction in the terrain, except for a large barn of Lord Erok which, at the time the fearsome combat was first engaged, still stood at the crest of a small rise to the north. Brightly shone the moon that night. This gave a nice luster like midday to objects below and unusually good visibility for the classic and legendary conflict that was to follow.

While accounts by historians, bards and Sir George himself have often differed in their telling, all of this was witnessed by Nicholas, who had accompanied Sir George to the field of combat and whose report of the incident has proven to be the most reliable and believable account. You, however, may believe whatever you like.

Sir George trudged up the hill toward the barn, slogging his way through knee-deep snow. Behind him, at the bottom of the hill, sat that Nicholas fellow in his sleigh.

Blast him! George thought. If the meddlesome young man had not interfered at the Mary Krispnes Inn, I might have hidden there all night and not have had to come out here at all.

Sir George the Dragonslayer was a most handsome knight, as everyone knew, especially George. He looked fabulous in his armor, the ladies all swooned at his smile and he was an especially good dancer at feasts and balls. He had cultivated his swagger and his image and his manners until he was the darling of every lady and maid who visited the court of Duke and Duchess Wenceslas.

He might have been the perfect knight if it were not for the fact that he hated fighting.

Oh, he was outwardly willing to engage in tournaments and feats of strength but in truth each joust or arms demonstration made his stomach nervous. Accidents in these contests were common and he had perfected his own 'act of contrition' which in his case meant feigning feeling sad at harming his opponent and running off to 'recover from his remorse' when in fact his was losing his breakfast at the sight of his opponent's blood. When he was harmed, however, he promptly fainted – a common occurrence for him – and the ladies-in-waiting would care for him under the impression that his romantic sensibilities had gotten the better of him.

He had carefully cultivated the image of being the greatest knight in the world but now his reputation had caught up with him.

Since that Nicholas youth had so obligingly ruined his initial plan to hide out at the Mary Krispnes Inn, his only hope at this point was to make for Lord Erok's Barn at the crest of the hill and find a place to hide among the cows and the hay. Getting there, however, was proving difficult. The wonderland of snow was also very deep and it made for slow going for the knight in his armor. Real knights roast in the summer and freeze in the winter making the profession far less glamorous in reality than stories would lead you to believe. At the moment he was afraid of sticking his tongue out for fear of it freezing to the faceplate of his helmet.

His greatest hope was that Nicholas would give up and go away before any REAL dragon showed up – for Sir George the Dragonslayer was more terrified of dragons than anything else in the entire world.

Vronk flew over the tops of the forest trees in a depth of misery that he had not yet known in his young dragon lifetime.

Vronk was approaching his one hundredth Hatchling Day and, as such, knew that he had to earn his Dragon Name soon. The other dragons were already beginning to wag their forked tongues about how Vronk never seemed to take any initiative in getting his Naming Quest completed. Sure, he was extremely attentive in cooking class – where he excelled at glazes – and his skills in art and ceramics earned him high marks. Yet he had failed ferocity class three times in a row and it was said he only passed because Dorimanger the Wise had interceded on his behalf.

Then there was the whole question of fire breathing.

It was a terrible embarrassment to Vronk. Whenever he got overly excited or nervous he would develop a sudden case of hiccoughs. He would then belch fire from his mouth in uncontrollable burps from time to time until he calmed down. Some of the younger dragons found this hysterically funny. They made a cruel game of sneaking up behind Vronk and then either roaring or banging pots together. This would always result in a startled Vronk hiccoughing balls of flame that bounded about the cavern. The young dragons would scamper away laughing while the elder dragons, who were not amused by the irritating blasts, scolding Vronk, telling him he needed to be more careful or learn some self discipline. Vronk was always mortified when this happened but just couldn't seem to help himself. Dorimanger had even taken him aside and tried to comfort him, telling Vronk that his talent for making flame would eventually be a good thing and something he could be proud of later in life, but mostly Vronk just tried not to be too upset and keep his flame to himself.

But now Vronk was on his Naming Quest – on Midwinter's Eve of all nights – and having to face a fearsome and terrible creature called a 'knight' which everyone knew was the worst thing that any dragon could face. They were small and pointy and tricky and probably magical.

Vronk felt his stomach lurch. He tried to remember his ferocity class lessons but was drawing a complete blank. He gnawed at his talons as he flew, growing more nervous by the moment. He was quickly coming to the edge of the forest and could see the moon on the crest of the new-fallen snow stretching eastward to the human village and the more terrible castle beyond it.

It was then that he spied the large barn on the hilltop just ahead of him and a thought of some hope sprang into his head. The little dragon who had not yet earned his name flew directly toward the dark structure below him as quickly as he could. He decided that perhaps it was just big enough for him to hide behind until the knight gave up looking for him.

He was worried that it might upset the cows inside the barn but it was a risk he was willing to take.

After all, Vronk was more frightened at that thought of meeting an actual knight than anything else in the entire world.

Nicholas sat in his sleigh watching the knight trudge up the slope toward the barn trying to decide whether to put Sir George on his list or not.

"What do you think Dasher?" Nicholas asked one of the two reindeer lolling in the harness at the front of the sleigh.

Dasher shook his head, casting a suddenly flurry of ice and snow from his antlers.

"I can't decide either," Nicholas continued. The young man shifted in the sleigh, pulling his large coat tighter around him. He had long been in the habit of making lists about the people that he met in a small, bound book that he kept in his coat pocket. He had many different kinds of lists, his 'polite and rude' list, his 'merry and dismal' list and his 'joyful and bleak' list. Tonight he was contemplating a new kind of list and Sir George would be at the top of the negative side. "Have we ever met a man with more wind and less sail?"

Dancer trumpeted once then snorted.

"Well, you're right about that," Nicholas agreed. "I don't think this knight could take a cow in a fair fight let alone an actual dragon. I just hope he doesn't get himself killed first. It wouldn't do any of us any good if..."

A great shadow fell over Nicholas, the sleigh and the reindeer, blocking out the great disk of the moon. Nicholas looked up and saw the shadow of the dragon against the star-filled sky.

It was heading right toward the barn.

"Holly Berries!" Nicholas shouted, grabbing the reigns and urging his reindeer forward. Dasher and Dancer both pulled hard, picking up speed slowly through the snow as they plunged up the slope toward the crest of the hill. They heard a girlish scream then...

An enormous ball of flame exploded at the top of the hill. Nicholas felt its heat wash over him as the enormous fireball roiled into the sky. Through the rumbling roar of the conflagration he could hear the bellowing of cattle, the snapping of timbers and the hiss of melting snow flashing to steam. Nicholas whistled again to his team urging them fast up the slope directly toward the conflagration.

As they crested the ridge, Nicholas slowed his team to a halt and leapt from the sleigh.

There, lying face first in the snow, arms spread wide to either side, was Sir George. Moving and mooing all around the knight was the entire herd of Lord Erok's cattle, moments before having stampeded from the barn into the deep snow and now milling about in panicked confusion. The barn itself was burning fiercely, the roof having already collapsed into the inferno and one wall threatening to follow.

Towering over what remained of the bard stood a dragon on its hind legs, scooping up snow from the ground as quickly as it could and throwing it onto the fire, a panicked look in its large, emerald eyes. The dragon continued moving about the barn, throwing snow onto the blaze and seemed to be making some progress against the inferno when it saw Nicholas.

The dragon froze, staring at the human in the crimson colored coat.

Nicholas froze staring back at the dragon He swallowed hard, determined to help the townsfolk in Betwixt as he had promised. Nicholas drew in a deep breath and tried make his words sound more confident than he felt.

"Are you going to eat me, dragon?" Nicholas asked.

"Eat you? What a notion!" the dragon snorted out a puff of smoke as he spoke. "Dragons don't eat humankind – at least not on purpose. Whoever told you that was..."

The dragon stopped, his emerald eyes growing even wider as he stared at the red-clothed human with the dark hair standing below him.

"You speak <u>dragon</u>?" he asked, astonishment creeping into his rumbling voice.

"Not especially," Nicholas shrugged. "I <u>do</u> speak to animals. It's a gift I was given on a Yuletide some time ago, but that's a long story for another time. So you say that dragon's don't eat humans."

"Not on purpose," the dragon corrected, holding up a talon to make his point.

"Of course, my mistake," Nicholas nodded with a slight bow. "But you DO eat cows, do you not?"

"Oh, yes!" the dragon nodded enthusiastically. "Especially for the Midwinter's Feast! They are especially good roasted with a nice apple and cherry glaze. It's something of a specialty of mine, actually, which..."

"Roasted with a glaze?" Nicholas asked. It was his turn to be astonished. "I thought you just gobbled them up whole when you snatched them from the fields."

"Raw?" The dragon's snout screwed up in disgust. "Ew, yuck!"

"My apologies again," Nicholas said. "It's just that when you burned down the barn I assumed that..."

"If this is your barn," the dragon suddenly stammer, "I am SO sorry! I didn't mean to ... I mean, I didn't see the knight until I landed and he really startled me and..."

Nicholas held up his hand. The dragon managed to stop talking for a moment. Nicholas walked among the cattle and knelt down next to the knight.

"Did I hurt him?" the dragon asked wringing his fore paws together, his claws clacking in concern.

Nicholas rolled the knight over in the snow with some effort and opened the faceplate of his helmet. Sir George groaned.

"You did not hurt him," Nicholas said, much to the dragon's relief. "He's just fainted again. He'll be fine."

The remains of the barn collapsed into a burning heap. "But your barn..."

"It isn't my barn," Nicholas said, "but I do know the man who built it. Did you let these cattle out of the barn?"

"I had to let them out!" the dragon exclaimed. "They couldn't stay inside!"

"Of course not," Nicholas nodded. "That was most considerate of you. What is your name, dragon?

"Oh, I don't have a name yet," the dragon answered. "That's why I'm here."

"Ah!" Nicholas nodded without really understanding. "So what do the other dragons <u>call</u> you?"

"Vronk," the dragon replied.

"Well, Vronk," Nicholas asked. "Why have you come burning down barns, save the cows and make knights faint this Yuletide Eve?"

"Oh! That's easy!" Vronk said cheerfully. The dragon dropped the snow on the remaining flames of the barn. This final avalanche both dowsed the fire and collapsed the final wall into a splintered heap. "I want to take the head of the knight back to the cavern of King Quarg ... so that I can get my name!"

This, too, was of some confusion to Nicholas. "I'm not sure I understand."

"Dragons don't get their REAL names until they have gone on their Naming Quest," Vronk explained. "Until they prove their bravery and ferocity before the dragon clans they just have their common name. This is <u>my</u> Naming Quest ... to bring back the head of a knight so that we can leave our caverns and start hunting again for food."

"That's most interesting, since the knight here was going to bring your head to HIS king," Nicholas replied from among the cattle that were now getting mired in the snow. "Do you suppose that my head would do just as well?"

The dragon thought for a moment. Vronk leaned down and took a closer look at the human in the red long coat. "Are you going to be tricksy? I've heard that humans were often clever and tricksy."

"I may be jolly and quick but I've never been thought of as particularly tricksy," Nicholas replied with a nod of his head. "Perhaps if I wore the helmet, King Quag wouldn't know the difference,

He reached down to remove the plumed helmet from Sir George's head.

Suddenly the earth shook beneath Nicholas' feet as a dreadful trumpeting roar filled the air. The cattle panicked, stampeding once again, plunging in all directions through the deep snow. Dash and Dancer grunted loudly then fled back down the slope. Nicholas lost his balance, falling backward into the snow next to the still unconscious Sir George as the snow that lay on the ground around kicked up into an instant, howling gale. I was impossible to see anything that was happening around him. He had the horrible feeling that he was inside one of the snow globes he often liked to give at Yuletide and being shaken furiously.

Chapter 5:
The Cow's Tale

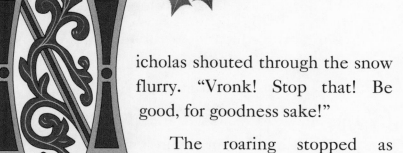

icholas shouted through the snow flurry. "Vronk! Stop that! Be good, for goodness sake!"

The roaring stopped as suddenly as it began. The ground stopped rolling as well and the blizzard that had sprung up around him softened as the flurry drifted slowly to the ground. Nicholas sat up, shaking the snow from his head and face, wishing -- and not for the first time -- that he had a nice beard to protect him from the cold. He took a deep breath.

The cows, however, were taking somewhat longer to calm down. They had stopped plowing through the snow but the cattle were still lowing.

The enormous face of Vronk emerged from the softly falling snow, his large emerald eyes narrowed as he squinted suspiciously at Nicholas. Smoke drifted menacingly from the dragon's nostrils. "You ARE tricksy! I saw you trying to take that iron mask off of the knight so that he could paralyze me with his horrible face and magical evil eye!"

"Sir George?" Nicholas scoffed. "Nonsense!"

"King Quarg told us all about knights!" Vronk snorted, blowing sulfurous smelling smoke out his snout. "All you humans are tricksy AND dangerous!"

The snow had settled around them. Nicholas stood up, put both his mitten-covered fists against this hip and faced the dragon with indignation. "You say humans are dangerous? Who made the knight faint? Who forced all these nice, innocent cows out of their comfortable barn? And who burned down their barn so they have no shelter and will probably freeze to death out here on MIdwinter's Eve?"

Vronk sat back on his tail and he looked around. Smoke curled up from the charred ruins of the barn. Cattle stood scattered all over the snow-blanketed hilltop, the snow trampled by their hooves in all directions and their mournful complaints rising into the night. The knight lay motionless in the snow. The features on the dragon's face softened from anger into remorse.

"A nice dragon like you making such a mess on Midwinter's Eve," Nicholas shook his head in disapproval. "If there's anything I know, it's naughty and nice! Now why would such a nice dragon like you do such a naughty thing?"

Vronk snuffled. His leathery wings sagged behind him and his head bent down. He looked away from Nicholas as he spoke. "I'm sorry. I didn't mean to make such a mess. It was an accident."

Nicholas dropped his hands next to his sides and sighed. "An accident, Vronk? Still, even if you didn't mean it, you have caused quite a lot of trouble. What are you going to do about it?"

Vronk towered over Nicholas, twisting his head in puzzlement. "Do about it?"

"Yes, you need to make things better," Nicholas said casually. "How to you feel right now about what you've done to these cattle?"

"Terrible," Vronk replied, resisting a sudden urge to gnaw at his talon.

"You would like to feel better about depriving these cows of their shelter on a cold winter's night," Nicholas continued, "wouldn't you?"

"Very much," Vronk replied.

"Then what do you think you need to do?" Nicholas asked.

The dragon considered for a while as he sat in the snow. The night was getting deeper and much colder but Nicholas was a patient man.

"Well," Vronk said at last. "You can talk to animals. You could tell the cattle how sorry I am for burning down their home."

"That is a very good idea," Nicholas agreed, stroking his chin thoughtfully and wishing again for a beard. "One should always apologize when they do something wrong but in many cases -- especially this one -- it won't help much."

Vronk leaned forward, dropping to rest again on all four of his paws. He craned his neck around so that he could see Nicholas better. "Why not?"

"Well, to be perfectly honest – and I am <u>always</u> as honest as possible under every circumstance," Nicholas admitted, "the usefulness of speaking to animals often depends upon the animal with whom you are trying to speak. You and I, for example, are having a rather wonderful conversation out here in the freezing night when we should both be attending to our celebration feasts in warmer and more comfortable surroundings. Cows, on the other hand, are a different story."

Vronk cast a skeptical look at the diminutive Nicholas standing in the snow beneath him. "You seem to use more words confusing words when you're trying to be honest."

"I did say <u>perfectly</u> honest," Nicholas noted. "Being perfect at something sometimes requires a lot more explaination."

"So you should be perfectly clear with the cows that I'm sorry for burning down their home," Vronk said.

"It will not do any of us much good," Nicholas said.

"I would like you to try all the same," Vronk insisted.

"Very well," Nicholas shrugged. "For your sake, I will try."

Nicholas turned to the nearest bovine standing several yards away. He pushed through the deep snow as close as he dared and spoke. The cow before him raised its head and turned to face Nicholas then turned away again.

The conversation was exceedingly brief.

Nicholas returned through the snow to where Vronk waited in expectation.

"Well, what did you say to the cow?" Vronk asked.

"I told the cow that you were sorry for having burned down his barn, that you regret your actions have inadvertently brought this dire problem to each of them individually and that you would appreciate the herd accepting your deepest regrets," Nicholas answered.

"And what did the cow say in response?" Vronk continued.

"Moo," Nicholas responded.

"Moo?" The dragon blinked in puzzlement.

"The cow said, 'Moo,'" Nicholas affirmed. "All I claimed was that I could talk to the animals, not that all animals would have anything meaningful to say. There's just not a great deal going on when it comes to cow's thoughts and conversation."

The legs of the dragon gave way beneath him and he fell suddenly to the ground, causing another flurry of snow to fly into the air.

"It's probably just as well," Nicholas said in comforting tones. "The cows don't need an apology ... they need a place to shelter for the night."

Vronk lifted up his head, a smile playing over his sharp teeth. "Shelter! There's one of those 'barns' you talk about south of here! I saw it when I was flying over the forest."

"Of course! Lord Ayhard's sheep pens," Nicholas agreed. "Yes, the cattle should shelter nicely there and Ayhard certainly won't be around to complain about it tonight. I'm sure that he'll be up at the castle complaining there about something else instead. But these cattle cannot possibly get that far through this deep snow tonight."

"Of course they can!" Vronk said. "Wait right here!"

The dragon hunched down into the snow and then vaulted into the sky, spreading its leathery wings and blocking out most of the stars. One great downward sweep created a gust of wind and a tempest of snow around Nicholas. In the next moment the shadow of the dragon was rising higher into the sky, rushing to the west toward the forest and the mountains.

Nicholas stood still for a moment in the quiet stillness of the Yuletide night. There was a quiet beauty to it all which he wished he could appreciate. He had all his baking to do this evening and deliveries yet to make to the homes across the countryside. At least there were a few things he could do while he waited. Nicholas whistled loudly and, within a few moments, could see Dancer and Dasher returning up the slope with his sled in tow. Both of the reindeer began complaining at once but it was Dancer who was the most annoyed.

"There's no need for language like that," Nicholas scolded. He reached down and started removing the armor from the knight. "We've got work to do and not much time before the dragon comes back."

Dasher bleated his concern while shaking his antlers.

"Yes, we have to save the knight, too," Nicholas explained as he yanked the helmet from Sir George's head. "The blankets in the back of the sled will keep him far warmer than this armor and we need him alive."

Dancer and Dasher both grunted and stomped at the same time.

"Why?" Nicholas exclaimed as he yanked off one of Sir George's steel gloves. "Because we need him if we're going to save this holiday for everyone. It's far better to have Sir George here as a living, lying cad than a martyred, silent knight!"

Good Duke Wenceslas looked out on the beastly season.

The Duke and Duchess – and for that matter, nearly everyone from the court who could possibly fit

– stood on the wide balcony that looked out from Wenceslas' keep westward toward the town of Betwixt. There was another winter storm gathering over the mountains and the Duke knew that there would be snowfall by morning but for now the stillness of the air allowed everyone to see as far as the edge of the forest in the distance.

"Is it not as I told you, My Lord?" Lord Erok intoned with as much dramatic solemnity as he could muster. His performance suffered from the chattering of his teeth although it was only marginally colder on the balcony than in the hall they had just left. "It is a battle worthy of an epic poem that shall be told down through the ages and with which your name shall forever be immortalized!"

"A conflict worthy of a song!" Lord Ayhard agreed.

"It would appear so," Wenceslas nodded as he shivered. The explosion and sudden flames in the distance had brought the guards on watch scurrying into the hall with the news. The Duke has arrived on the balcony moments later to witness for himself the conflagration in the distance until it had been inexplicably extinguished. "Do you not have a barn near that place, Lord Erok?"

"Yes, My Lord," Lord Erok intoned, "although given the epic nature of the conflict at hand and how its telling shall grace your court, I am confident that any rightful destruction caused by your knight will be justly compensated by your most gracious..."

"Yes, Lord Erok!" The Duke often tired of Lord Erok's long speeches but the chill had made them particularly wearing this night. "If my knight burned down your barn, I'll pay for another to be built."

"I should point out that it was an exceptionally LARGE barn," Lord Erok said with a slight bow. "Its workmanship rivaled many of the finest houses and the cost of replacing it will be unusually high."

"When have I ever known you to do anything that did not have an exceptionally high cost, Lord Erok?" The Duke sniffed. "I should like to hear from Sir George, however, before we settle on any damages..."

"My Lord!" interrupted Lord Ayhard. "Look!"

Everyone on the balcony gasped.

In the distance near where Lord Erok's increasingly large and magnificent barn had so recently lit up the horizon, an explosion of snow burst upward from the landscape. It continued toward the south, a succession of enormous crystal-white plumes bursting into the wintery sky hundreds of feet into the air.

"Sir George is pushing the dragon southward!" exclaimed Lord Erok.

"But... that's toward MY barn!" howled Lord Ayhard.

"A barn that is nearly as glorious as my own once was," intoned Lord Erok, nudging Ayhard with his elbow, "as we shall mutually attest. Our just and fair compensation for their loss would be nothing to the coffers of Duke Wenceslas in exchange for the glorious battle now being waged on his behalf by the undaunted Sir George the Dragonslayer!"

"Fight on, brave Sir George!" Ayhard shouted a moment later when understood Lord Erok's meaning.

It was a wondrous holiday parade that took place that night although, sadly, only the cows were close enough to properly observe it and they, as we now know, were quite incapable of appreciating it.

First leading the procession strode the dragon that was barely into his scales pushing forward through the snow so low that its breast was pushing the drifts aside almost as though Vronk were swimming through them. Behind him, the dragon's tail was wrapped around the trunks of three evergreen trees whose branches splayed out behind him forming a great plow. As the dragon pressed forward, he dragged the trees behind him, the deep snow billowing up on either side high into the air as it carved a wide swath through the snow.

Next, between the plumes of snow came a rather nervous pair of reindeer pulling behind them a small sleigh burdened only with Nicholas – who did not then weigh nearly as much as he would later in life – and Sir George. The knight did not weigh nearly as much at this point either as he had been stripped of all his magnificent armor and wet outer garments. Now he was resting comfortably under stacks of thick quilts and blankets clad only in his winter underwear.

Finally, following the occasional call from Nicholas, came the herd of Lord Erok's cattle, trudging along the newly-formed road before them as they all progressed toward Lord Ayhard's sheep pens. In a very short time, the cow-pageant arrived at Lord Ayhard's sheep pens. Nicholas opened the rather modest barn which was not nearly as magnificent as Lord Ayhard was remembering it to the Duke at that moment and the cattle were contented for the night once more.

Vronk lay down for a moment at the north-west corner of the sheep pens. The sheep were bunched very tightly in the south-east corner as Nicholas closed the door to the barn.

"That was a wonderful idea," Nicholas commented to the dragon. "The cows are grateful ... well, as grateful I suppose as cows can ever be ... and you're looking a good deal happier!"

"I am happier," Vronk said with a contented sigh that involved a puff of sulfurous smoke that rather terrified the sheep at the other corner of the pen. "In fact, I feel better than I ever have before on a Midwinter's Eve."

"Indeed?" Nicholas' laugh was deep and hearty. "I feel this way EVERY Midwinter's Eve."

"You do?" The dragon raised his head from the snow in astonishment. "Why?"

"It's a sort of magic," Nicholas chuckled. "But I can teach it to you – in fact, you've already started to learn it."

"I have?" the dragon blinked his emerald eyes as he reached up with a talon from his right claw and scratched at one of his horns.

"Yes, and you're doing very well at it, too," Nicholas continued as he climbed back into his sleigh. "Now, if you'll follow me, I'll teach you some more of this magic."

"I thought we were going back to Quarg's cavern?" Vronk said suspiciously. "I'm supposed to bring back the head of a knight!"

"We are and you will," Nicholas nodded, taking up the reigns, "but first I want to teach you this magic. You DO want to learn the magic and feel this way every Midwinter's Eve, don't you?"

"Yes," Vronk nodded his massive head.

"Then we're headed back to Betwixt," Nicholas said.

"Should you check on your captured knight?" Vronk asked.

"No, I can see that he is sleeping and believe me, I'd know if he were awake," Nicholas replied. "Come follow me, Vronk, and drag those trees with you!"

"Your Grace!" exclaimed Lord Erok as he pointed toward his land holdings to the south west. "The battle has been taken up yet again!"

Duke Wenceslas looked out once more. The great clouds of white billowed upward from the ground once more into the sky.

"They are moving again, My Lord!" cried Lord Ayhard who was feeling somewhat disappointed that his own barn had not apparently been burned down so fortuitously as his neighbor's. "They're ... they appear to be bringing their fight directly toward Betwixt!"

"Call out the guard!" ordered the Duke. "Assemble the bowmen and the pikemen as well. We may have to join Sir George in his battle with the dragon in order to save the village!"

"Hold a moment, my dearest," said the Duchess. "See? The billows have stopped again outside of the town."

Something from across the distance to Betwixt then caught the ear of Wenceslas.

"What is that sound?" The Duke asked, straining toward the distant sound.

"I should gladly form a commission at once to investigate any sound that Your Grace should be hearing!" volunteered Lord Erok loudly.

"Silence!" Wenceslas demanded.

He turned his ear slightly to the west.

"Is that wood chopping I hear?"

Chapter 6:
The Mouse's Tale

etwixt was in a complete panic! From the moment young Miss Ellie Tow, daughter of old Stubby Tow, went out to churn the butter and saw Vronk approaching in a great flurry of snow from the west, she had run down through the village screaming at the top of her lungs that the dragon was coming to eat them all for Yuletide. Within moments, everyone in Betwixt knew what had to be done; they formed a mob with pitchforks, scythes, axes, clubs and lanterns to go out and meet the threat in disorganized panic. This was their birthright as villagers and they instinctively knew to put their mob into action before anyone with authority or organizational ability could react with reason and spoil the opportunity for a perfectly good riot. Rupert, sensing that this was the moment for revolution, quickly grabbed a bed sheet and brandished it as a flag, crying out for everyone to 'mount the barricades' even though there were no barricades available.

Much to Rupert's disappointment, the uprising he was hoping for was not to be. Nicholas was approaching the town in front of the dragon and seeing the assembling mob, the young man stopped his sleigh and instructed the dragon to wait while he addressed the fierce-looking villagers.

Nicholas spoke up as he trudged through the snow and approached the panicked townsfolk. "What a wonderful, warm greeting! I want to thank you all for coming out to welcome us..."

"What happened to the knight?" Jim Frist demanded.

"Oh, he's in the back of the sleigh," Nicholas said with a smile. "He'll be all right although the encounter didn't go exactly as he had hoped."

"So you brought the DRAGON back with you as well?" Two-ton Tim yelled.

"Yes, but he's only a small one," Nicholas said, "and very pleasant once you get to know him."

"The only good dragon is a slain dragon!" snapped Old Man Winters. "Let's recklessly charge him in an irrational and unprovoked attack!"

"Why?" demanded Mary Krispnes who was awkwardly holding both a pitchfork and a lantern at the same time.

"It's tradition!" answered Old Man Winters with pride.

"He's right! We're being repressed!" Rupert shouted, waving his bed sheet.

"I'm getting out my list!" Nicholas shouted, reaching inside his great crimson coat. Subtlety had not worked and, in those desperate times, Nicholas was not above threats. He pulled out a small, leather bound collection of velum. His pencil hovered over the pages as he glared at the mob of townsfolk.

The people in Betwixt drew in a collective breath and took a step back.

No weapon was more effective in that moment than a black mark on Nicholas's fruitcake gifting list.

"It's Yuletide Eve!" Nicholas bellowed, his deep, commanding voice roaring over the crowd. "It's the night of PEACE and JOY and GOODWILL ... and we're going to have peace, joy and goodwill if I have to put coal in every person's stocking here!"

"Actually," Mary Krispnes pointed out, "coal would be a pretty good gift."

"I was only threatening in metaphor," Nicholas said, forcing himself to calm down. "Now, this dragon came with a Yuletide gift for everyone in Betwixt tonight and you're all going to put down those pitchforks and accept his gift and you had better be nice to this dragon! I'll know if you've been bad or good... so be GOOD, or else!"

"What gift could a dragon possible bring Betwixt?" Old Man Winters demanded.

Nicholas turned toward Vronk and signaled him with his gloved hand.

Vronk shifted sideways, pulling his tail around ... and with it the three enormous trees he had brought from the Western Forest.

"His name is Vronk," Nicholas said to the mob in Betwixt, "and he hopes his gift helps make your Yuletide a bit more joyful and warm."

Vronk was startled when all the woodsmen from the town rushed forward with their axes in hand. He was about to launch into his 'Basic Ferocious Dance #3' – the only one which he had properly learned in Ferocious Class and the one he had performed earlier that same night when he had feared Nicholas was going to expose the knights deadly eye – but Nicholas signaled him to wait. It turned out that the woodsmen were not intent on attack the dragon but were instead intent on attacking the felled trees. In short order the wood was being distributed to the very happy citizens in Betwixt with fires being kindled in every fireplace nook of the town.

However, as happy as the people in Betwixt were that night to finally have fires to grace their hearths, it was the aromas that were soon drifting from the homes that made the dragon's head reel with delight.

Vronk breathed in so deeply that Nicholas's sleigh was dragged, over the protest of the reindeer, a few feet across the snow toward the dragon. "What is that marvelous smell?"

Nicholas looked up from his sleigh, drew in his own breath and smiled. "Ah! That is my fruitcake! It seems that the ovens are already working."

"Ovens!" Vronk exclaimed, his thunderous voice nearly shaking loose several squares of glass from their window glazing. "You mean, you do BAKING in Betwixt?"

"Why, yes," Nicholas admitted. "Baking at Yuletide is a tradition among us."

"Oh, baking!" Vronk's voice seemed to catch with emotion as he spoke the word. "Dragons have longed to know about this ... this baking! We have for many centuries enjoyed the roasting skills, of course, and have perfected the arts of marinade, sauces and gravies although the shaping of our cookware remains somewhat difficult as it is all made by us from stone. We have even experimented with grains and eggs but we have never been able to duplicate the concept of this mystical thing you call ovens into anything that works."

"Couldn't you ask the dwarves to build ovens for you?" Nicholas asked in surprise. "They're quite good at it."

"Dragons have never been able to get close enough to a dwarf to ask one," Vronk admitted.

"Well, then, I must introduce you to my fruitcake," Nicholas smiled. He clucked at Dasher and Dancer, who drew the sled forward onto the wide village street. "Come with me! I want to show you something."

It was most fortunate that Vronk, as was mentioned before, was a small dragon although relative to the streets in Betwixt he was still very large indeed. He barely managed to follow Nicholas as the crimson-clothed human led him down the streets of the town. In each lane the snow was glistening. Warm lights spilled from the windows as house after house stoked their fires and pushed back the winter chill. Vronk managed to peak in through these windows and saw humans in what he realized were their diminutive 'mountainless-caves' smiling, laughing and content in the warms spilling from their hearth.

Vronk's smile was deepening. "Did we do this?"

Nicholas laughed. "No ... YOU did this."

"I only brought them a few trees," Vronk rumbled.

"You brought them what they needed," Nicholas shrugged. "It may not have been much to you but it was everything to them. Moving a single stone can cause a river to change its course. Sometimes the greatest of changes are accomplished with the smallest investment of a well placed gift. Ah, here we are!"

"Here we are ... where?" the dragon asked, squeezing his bulk carefully between the buildings and trying not to step on anything that might break in the rather fragile world of humans that suddenly surrounded him.

"This is the Mary Krispness Inn," Nicholas announced. "The finest public house and the best ovens in all of Betwixt." Nicholas announced. He stepped from the sleigh just as a number of his friends within the Inn called 'Yoo-hoo!' Nicholas smiled and waved to them. "Tim! Bill! Come give me a hand with our old friend Sir George!"

Tim and Bill stepped out of the door to the Inn but stopped cold when they saw the dragon filling the street outside.

"Oh, he's all right," Nicholas said. "He's with me."

While this assurance did not entirely convince either Two-ton Tim or Bill Frist they nevertheless managed to force themselves out to the sleigh. There they found Sir George sprawled under the blankets with his mouth hanging open in a most unattractive manor.

"Bless us, every one! Is he dead as a doornail?" Two-ton Tim asked.

"No, just fainted is all," Nicholas said, waving his gloved hand dismissively. "Take him inside and put him near the hearth. Warm him up and I'm sure he'll come around just fine."

"But he aint got nothing on save his underclothes," Bill said, hauling the knight out over the edge of the sleigh. "How do you know it's the knight without his armor?"

"You know it's him when he wakes up and starts speaking," Nicholas nodded. "Meanwhile, I've got to show this dragon all about fruitcake!"

Two-ton Tim looked as though he were about to ask a question but decided at the last moment that he really did not want to know the answer. He and Bill

Frist grabbed a leg and an arm each of the stripped knight and dragged him in through the front door of the Inn. Nicholas and Vronk both heard the laughter from inside the Mary Krispnes Inn just before the door shut.

"Come around the back and I'll show you the ovens," Nicholas smiled as he urged the dragon to follow him.

Vronk squeezed himself tightly through the alley and into gratefully larger courtyard behind the Inn. There was a latticework window in the back of the Inn that looked inside to the large kitchen, one wall of which was occupied by banks of brick ovens all of which were in full use. Two long tables lay beneath the window, one covered in baking forms filled with a most interesting looking batter and the other already filling with finished brown loaves studded with brightly colored fruit.

"Baking!" the dragon breathed in wonder.

"Wait here and I'll be right back," Nicholas said. He opened the back door to the kitchen. Suddenly, the warm, sweet smell of baking drifted out of the doorway and directly into Vronk's nostrils.

The dragon's eyes went suddenly wide. Tears began to form in his eyes which, were you there to collect them, would have been most valuable indeed. Vronk's lower lip began to quiver over his sharp, long teeth and he suddenly forgot all about gnawing on his talons. He forgot in that instant all about his Naming Quest, King Quarg and his mission to bring back the head of a knight.

It was the most incredible, delicious and desirable smell he had ever experienced.

Vronk knew that he would give anything to possess his very own fruitcake.

"The dragon is in the village, sire!" Lord Ayhard yelled.

"I'm standing right here, Ayhard!" The Duke winced at the sudden noise in his ear. "I can see for myself that the dragon is in Betwixt. The question is what is it doing there?"

"Isn't it obvious?" Lord Erok blurted out. "I mean, Your Grace, can you not see the smoke rising from the town?"

"Yes, I believe I can," Duke Wenceslas grumbled. "Where is Sir George? What is he up to?"

Sir George, the sleeping knight, awoke with a start. He flailed about, casting his blankets off in the sudden fear that he was somehow being held by monster, which is why, when he came to his senses, he was staring back into the faces of the Inn patrons who were staring back at him as he staggered to his feet clad only in his underwear.

"Can I get you anything?" quipped Noel Tannenbaum, Mary Krispnes's barmaid who was casting a cool eye over the discomfited knight.

The patrons in the tavern laughed heartily.

"What happened?" Sir George demanded, hastily gathering up the blanket and covering himself up as best he could. "How did I get here? Where's the dragon?"

"Oh, it's the dragon you're wanting," Old Man Winters chuckled. "Well, I think we can help you there, sir knight. He's round back of the Inn ... through the kitchen, I believe."

"The dragon's in the <u>town</u>!" Sir George exclaimed. He was feeling decidedly woozy again. "You've got to kill it!"

"Rise up we shall!" cried Rupert, thrusting his fist into the air. "Rise up against the proletariat that enslaves the people! Down with governments! Up with dragons!"

"No! No!" Sir George said, shaking his head violently and instantly regretting it. "Someone's got to stop the dragon!"

"Why?" demanded Noel. "He aint hurtin' nothin'."

"Are you people all mad?" Sir George gaped. "We need an army to fight this terrible monster. I've got to get back to the castle!"

"Well, deary," Noel shrugged. "You're hardly presentable at court at the moment."

"But... but I've got to get back to the Duke at once!" Sir George begged.

"You can relax, love," Noel said, shaking her head at the pathetic knight as she tossed him a rough-cloth sack. "We figured you'd be needing some clothing. Took up a collection, we did."

So it was that within minutes, Sir George the Dragonslayer was back on the steed he had left at the Inn earlier in the evening, riding hard for Duke Wenceslas's castle. He wore a pair of old pants from Two-ton Tim, a stained frill blouse from Noel Tannenbaum, a scarf with the slogan 'Down with Authority' knitted into its pattern from Rupert, a shredded wool coat from Old Man Winters and a stocking cap with a bell for a tassel from Bill Frist. The farmer's boots were provided by Mary Krispnes from the Inns collection of lost items.

All Sir George left at the Inn were Nicholas' blankets and growing laughter at the memory of how the knight looked as he left.

Nicholas emerged from the back door of the Inn's kitchen with a number of the amazing fruitcake's in a large box. Vronk stared at him as loaded them into the back of his sleigh, barely daring to hope that one of them might be for him.

As Nicholas turned to go back into the kitchen, however, he stopped and suddenly leaned forward.

Vronk craned his neck around the sleigh, trying to see and suddenly stopped.

Nicholas was conversing with a mouse.

The dragon shivered. Creatures that were smaller than him always frightened Vronk and the sight of this truly diminutive animal made the dragon shudder. Gratefully, the mouse abruptly ran off.

Nicholas straightened and glanced up at the dragon. "We've got to go right away."

"You mean to Quarg's lair?" Vronk asked hopefully.

"No, I told you I have some deliveries to make first," Nicholas said, climbing into the sleigh and gathering up the reins at once, "and this one cannot wait."

Nicholas drove the sleigh out of Betwixt, northward down the old Empire Road. Vronk followed easily in the sky above, keeping an eye on Nicholas along the road as it wound next to the frozen river. As they came to a wide bend, Nicholas stopped and Vronk was obliged to land behind him.

"Why are we here?" Vronk asked Nicholas.

One of the reindeer snorted and kicked.

"That was rude, Dancer. Vronk does not know any better," Nicholas said to the reindeer, then pointed ahead of them to where the road curved near the river. "The mouse in town told me of this place. Mice generally speak too quickly to be understood and they never say much of interest except in the case of need. We have come here because of the mouse's tale. Can you see it, Vronk?"

Against the hillside near the road there was a home built into the hillside. This struck the dragon as a particularly smart arrangement on the part of the humans inside as at least this home was a partial cavern. Dragons always believe that it is much safer underground. Yet as he had come in the last few hours to become acquainted with the strange ways of humans, Vronk realized that there was something wrong with this particular home. They had brought cheery warmth to Betwixt but there was no warmth here save a single flickering flame that peeked between the warped slats of the door.

"Someone lives here on Yuletide Eve?" the dragon inquired in as quiet a voice as he could manage.

"Yes," said Nicholas. "A family who is struggling through the winter."

"Why do they not live with the other humans in Betwixt?" the dragon continued.

"They are poor," Nicholas answered with a heavy sigh.

"What is poor?" asked Vronk.

Nicholas pondered how he might answer the dragon in terms that the creature could understand. "Poor is not having when others have."

"Like your Lord Erok having the cattle," Vronk said, his eyes narrowing in thought. "And because he has the cattle other people cannot have them?"

"Something like that," Nicholas agreed.

"Dragons understand no such thing," Vronk sniffed in disapproval. "We take care of our clans and our kind. We do not withhold what others need."

Nicholas looked up at Vronk and thought for a moment before answering. "Humans could learn a

great deal from dragons. That is why we have come –
to share what we have with those who have not."

"What have you brought to share?" the dragon
asked.

"I've a few toys for their children," Nicholas said.

"Your toys will not keep them warm," Vronk
grumbled.

"I have brought them one of my fruitcakes,"
Nicholas offered.

"A gift worthy of a king," Vronk agreed, "but it
will not take the chill from their bones. We should
bring them wood to warm their cavern as we did in
Betwixt."

"And that I have brought, too," Nicholas replied.
"But it will not last them for very long."

Vronk thought for a moment then nodded. He
reached down with his right talons to his scales that
were changing from green to gold. He found one
beneath his wings in an obscure place that would not
be noticed. There he removed a small scale in
dragon's terms but measuring almost two feet across
when he handed it to Nicholas.

The man in the crimson coat nearly dropped the scale. It radiated tremendous warmth on its own and had Nicholas not been wearing his gloves, might have burned his hands.

"Have them place this in their hearth," Vronk said with a smile. "It will take care of them through the winter."

"Can you part with it?" Nicholas asked with a knowing smile.

"It means little to me and it means everything to them," Vronk said and then turned his head to look at Nicholas. "Dragons take care of their clans."

"Are these poor people, then, part of your clan?" Nicholas asked quietly in the winter's night. "Am I?"

"We are in the world together," Vronk mused.

The dragon turned his gaze toward the small hovel set in the hillside bend of the road. "I do not know these humans who live in such want but I wish to join my clan to theirs. Why should I not consider you or them part of a greater clan? These lords in the castle and the dragons in the mountains and these people in Betwixt or out of it for that matter ... could they not also be part of my clan, too? We should all be one clan, especially at Midwinter's Feast."

"Then, you have learned the Yuletide magic after all," Nicholas said as he climbed out of the sleigh, "I shall go visit this humble home and you, my friend, shall go back to the forest and bring some more of those trees. And as soon as you get back we're going to take care of all our clans – AND fulfill that Name Quest of yours!"

Chapter 7:
The Dragon's Tale

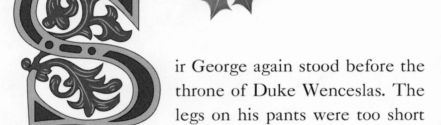

ir George again stood before the throne of Duke Wenceslas. The legs on his pants were too short and the waist was entirely too wide. He had found a length of hemp rope which he tied around the top of the pants to hold them up. The ruffled blouse was too small for him and the toggle strained across his chest to remain closed. The third toggle down from the top had failed utterly and so presented a perpetual gap showing his underwear between his belly and his chest. He was forced to continue wearing the shredded wool coat that only now he noticed reeked of Old Man Winter's smell and the stocking cap whose bell had the unfortunate tendency to tinkle brightly whenever his head shifted.

"Sir George the Dragonslayer," the Duke spoke the acknowledgement with a tone of doubt although whether the uncertainty was occasioned by the knight's appearance or performance one can only imagine. Duke Wenceslas gripped the rather beaten-up bundle of thyme in his hand and wondered how he was supposed to grant this award of courage to a knight so bizarrely dressed. Still, he felt he had no choice, and handed the tied sprigs over to the outstretched hand of the knight.

"My Lord," Sir George said, bowing with a flourish although the depth of his obeisance was cut short when the rope around his pants threatened to give way.

"Your appearance is ... much altered since we saw you last," noted the Duchess with a smile playing at the corner of her lips.

"Indeed, it is, My Lord," Sir George nodded, his face flushing red. In addition to his other wardrobe issues, the boots were also too large for him and the laces missing so that they tended to clomp when he tried to walk across the floor. Holding the bundled sprigs of thyme did not enhance his appearance. "I fear that you do not see me at my best ... but the urgency of my mission demands that I forego propriety!"

"Urgent, indeed," the Duke said, his breath puffing out in great clouds into the frigid hall as he spoke. "Your quest has been urgent from the beginning. We have followed it with some concern. I trust you found the dragon?"

"Why, yes, sire!" Sir George nodded enthusiastically, his dark curls bouncing from beneath his cap and the bell tinkling with wild abandon. "On the west road approach to the forest, near Lord Erok's barn..."

"And was the combat epic?" the Duchess asked with words that sounded both sweet and sticky at the same time.

"Why ... yes, My Lord!" Sir George stammered.

"Then perhaps you might instruct us on why you have returned not only without the head of this dragon," Duke Wenceslas said as his eyes narrowed, "but without your own armor and clothing as well."

"Ah, yes, well," Sir George tried to find some foothold in the increasingly awkward and slippery conversation. "As the Duchess has surmised, the confrontation was, indeed, epic."

"Epic, indeed," Duke Wenceslas observed. "We watched much of it from our own battlements even to the point where the dragon entered Betwixt and threatened my citizens of that township."

"Indeed, My Lord," Sir George nodded, his hat ringing yet again. "Which is why we must call upon the forces of your army at once to..."

"I have already ordered them to assemble and we march within the hour," Duke Wenceslas interrupted. "But you, Sir George, can be of great help to us as we prepare our strategy for you alone have done combat with this monstrous creature."

"Sire," Sir George smiled and gave a practiced deprecating shrug. "I am but one humble knight in the service of your glorious reign. What happened between Erok's and Ayhard's place really isn't..."

"Indeed, tell us all what happened between Erok's and Ayhard's place?" the Duke insisted.

Sir George stammered, "But Your Grace..."

The Duke slightly emphasized each word as he leaned forward with a scowl. "Tell us."

"Well, it was a cold winter's night as I ... as I strode purposefully onto the field of conflict." Sir George swallowed hard.

"Go on," the Duke insisted.

"The snow was deep and crisp and even, as you know," Sir George licked his lips and then continued. He could see the ladies in waiting leaning forward in anticipation. "Brightly shone the moon tonight. I had left my steed in Betwixt, fearing that the impending presence of the dragon might drive my dear horse – battle-tried as he was – to madness. I leaped from the sleigh, my sword in hand..."

"Sleigh?" the Duchess asked. "What sleigh?"

"It was a sleigh which I had procured in town, demanding in Your Grace's name that the poor, frightened peasant take me at once into the very maw of danger," Sir George was warming to his subject despite the freezing air of the audience hall. "Every sense was heightened within me as I strode up the hill toward the barn. I knew instinctively that the dragon would be drawn in its mindless primal hunt toward Lord Erok's cattle. My intuition was confirmed, for there, swooping out of the darkness..."

"But wasn't the moon shining?" commented the Duchess.

"Swooping out of the moon-lit darkness," Sir George hastily amended, "came a dragon larger and more powerful than any I had ever encountered before. Malice exuded from every black scale of its ancient hide! Its eyes were filled with flame and its razor-like talons were shredding cattle for its own fiendish pleasure! Flames shout outward from the brimstone of its maw..."

"Is that when it burned down my barn?" Lord Erok asked breathlessly.

"It burned down? Oh, yes, of course," Sir George nodded. "The flames spewing from the dragon were so overwhelming that they consumed the barn, driving the cattle mad with fear. The monstrous creature was distracted at that moment, most likely by the cows running wild about its feet, so I gripped my sword and prepared to sneak up quietly..."

"In your armor?" the Duchess exclaimed. "How could you possibly sneak up on anything in your armor?"

"And what happened to your armor?" the Duke added.

"Ah! Therein is found the cunning craft of a dragon-slayer," Sir George said. His mouth was feeling a little dry in the freezing hall. "I quickly removed my armor, you see, setting it up as a clever subterfuge so that the dragon would think I was actually near the barn whilst I was stealthily maneuvering to attack it unknowingly from behind..."

"You say you took OFF your armor in order to attack the dragon?" the Duke exclaimed, his eyes narrowing. "And the dragon just sat there, waiting while you removed the helmet, the paldrons, the greaves and quisse and sabaton, the gauntlets and breastplate and chain mail and then stood still while you set all this up as some sort of armored scare-crow? And THEN did not notice while you tiptoed around his back through the snow with nothing but your boots, sword and winter woolies for protection?"

Sir George drew in a deep breath but could suddenly think of nothing to say.

"And so tell me, Sir George," the Duke's voice was menacingly quiet as he stood up from his throne and snatched the bundle of thyme back from the knight. "Where IS that dragon's head that you promised to bring me?"

A loud voice suddenly boomed through the frost-caked hall from the courtyard doors that were opening just wide enough at the far end of the hall. "It is here, Your Grace! I have brought the dragon's head!"

The Duke looked up in surprise. "Nicholas?"

The courtiers looked up in surprise. Nicholas was always expected on Yuletide Eve with his wondrous and magical tasting fruitcake but with the dragon trouble in Betwixt, few in the court actually believed that he would manage his deliveries this year. Now the young man stepped between the partially open great doors, his long crimson coat open in the front, showing off his beautiful doublet underneath. He removed his gloves despite the cold and bowed where he stood.

"I was there, Your Highness and witnessed the battle firsthand," Nicholas said, with a nod toward Sir George who stood working his mouth silently like a fish just pulled from the river. "I can tell you every detail of what happened there at Lord Erok's barn and at Lord Ayhard's sheep pens and, need I add, in the town of Betwixt afterward – but first I have someone with me who wishes to present you with a great gift, if the Duke is willing to accept it with grace and serenity."

"I shall do my best," the Duke chuckled. "Let him present his gift."

"Well, My Liege," Nicholas said, turning back toward the nearly-closed doors. "I told you I brought you the head of the dragon..."

He drew open the wide doors.

"...But I also brought the rest of the dragon with it."

The Duke leaped to his feet, standing protectively before the Duchess. The Lords stepped back in shock and surprise. The ladies-in-waiting did not wait another moment before running to the opposite end of the hall. The men-at-arms in the hall fumbled for their weapons.

The dragon calmly squeezed through the tall doors at the end of the hall then turned toward the massive hearth to one side of the room. To the astonishment of the court, the dragon dragged a tree into the hall with is tail. It carefully broke off the branches and splintered the trunk with its talon claws. Then it filled the great hearth with as much of the wood as it could hold. Pushing the rest of the shattered tree into the corner, the dragon squinted with one eye, making sure of his aim and then breathed out the narrowest stream of flame he could manage. The fire splayed into the firebox of the hearth, the wood bursting into flame with the warmth of it instantly spreading through the hall. The dragon continued its stream of inferno until wood blazed. The frost on the flagstones paving the floor of the hall evaporated. The ice crystals encasing the tall windows receded then vanished altogether. The Duchess sighed with joy and relief as she basked in the warmth filling the hall. Duke Wenceslas breathed in deeply and smiled, despite having a dragon taking up nearly half of his mammoth hall.

The dragon lowered his head, his gentle rumblings directed toward Nicholas who nodded at the sound.

"This creature speaks with you?" the Duke asked.

"Why is everyone so surprised by that?" Nicholas laughed. "Yes, he speaks to me."

"What does he say?" Duke Wenceslas asked.

"His name is Vronk and he wants to know if you have a cow for your feast," Nicholas replied. "He would very much like the honor of cooking it for you, providing your cooks would be willing to help with the glaze."

The Duke looked up in amazement and delight, nodding toward the dragon. Wenceslas held up to the dragon the bundle of thyme. "Please tell him that he is my champion."

Vronk looked down at the Duke with his large emerald eyes as he listened to Nicholas translate, carefully took the thyme between his claws and nodded in return.

"How is this possible?" the Duke asked Nicholas in wonderment.

"You would be surprised," Nicholas chuckled, "what you can get a dragon to do for fruitcake. But I do need a few favors of you, if I may, Your Grace."

"You have but to ask!" Duke Wenceslas said with cheer.

"First, I need three of Lord Erok's cattle," Nicholas said, "for a peace offering."

"It is as good as done," the Duke replied. "What other favor do you crave?"

"And I need you to grant me the title of 'knight'," Nicholas said quietly.

"You wish to be Sir Nicholas?" The Duke was astonished.

"Just for tonight," Nicholas insisted. "It's actually for a friend of mine."

Later that evening, Nicholas drove his sleigh westward toward the forest and the great mountains beyond. The winter storm had settled in and snowflakes were falling gently from the sky. Next to the sleigh walked Vronk, his wings folded back against his body and he kept pace with the sleigh and the reindeer pulling it.

"You realize that I have not finished my deliveries," Nicholas said to the dragon.

"And you realize that you would be able to complete your deliveries much quicker if you flew," the dragon replied.

"Flew?" Nicholas was astonished. "You must be joking!"

"Not at all," Vronk said casually. "Do you really think we dragons can remain in the sky on these wings alone? We use them mostly for moving about and changing direction of our flight ... but most animals can fly given the proper magic."

"I had no idea," Nicholas said. "What kinds of animals can fly?"

"Well, I wouldn't be so certain about cows, given what you've told me," Vronk chuckled deeply, "but I should think nearly any other animal could fly, even your reindeer, for example."

"What do you say to that, Dancer?" Nicholas laughed.

The reindeer snorted and bellowed loudly.

"Oh, I'm sure you could get use to it!" Nicholas chided, then turned back to Vronk. "I look forward to meeting your King, but I hope it won't take too long."

"Whatever happens," Vronk chuckled to himself. "I suspect your meeting will be brief!"

"At least you'll be honest when you present me to Quarg," Nicholas sighed. "It was good of the Duke to make me an official knight though I hardly feel like much of a hero."

"You are the best kind of hero," Vronk said as they moved into the forest with the great dragon mountains beyond. The dragon handed the bundle of thyme to a surprised Nicholas. "You're a clan-friend to all, and to me, a good knight."

Chapter 8: Dragonhearth

ountless years away and miles unnumbered, the stout old man with the great beard of flowing white sat back in his chair before the fading fire of the Griffin's Tale Inn, folded his arms across his ample chest and waited for the Dragonsbard to speak.

"But... the dragon," Edvard sputtered. "Sir Nicholas was going with Vronk back to the very lair of the dragons to have his head presented as a knight before the Dragon King!"

"Why so he was!" The older man furrowed his brow in thought then he turned toward Abel and gave the scribe a rather jolly wink.

"So what happened?" the bard demanded with urgency.

The older man pulled himself up out of the chair with a groan. He moved closer to the dying fire to warm his hands. "Nicholas went with Vronk westward that night and even rode on his back into the great mountains and Quarg's cavern. There, true to his word, he had his head presented to King Quarg. As with Duke Wenceslas, Vronk presented not only the 'head of a knight' but the rest of him as well. The assembled dragons in Quarg's cavern nearly went into a frenzy of fear until Vronk showed them true bravery by doing his 'Ferocious Dance #6' right in front of Sir Nicholas. Nicholas then offered the three cattle to Quarg as coming from Duke Wenceslas with the promise not to send any more knights to slay any further dragons. Then Vronk presented King Quarg with one of Nicholas' fruitcakes and all enmity disappeared. Quarg gave the confection a dragon name right then and there, which is interpreted as 'Midwinter Dragonbites', and promised peace with the humans of Wenceslasia if they would please share their secrets of baking and the mysteries of maintaining a proper oven temperature. Vronk actually took a job in the castle of Duke Wenceslas, being appointed the first official Dragonhearth of the realm and in charge of heat and roasting for all feasts. In time, Vronk brokered a wonderful peace between Wenceslas, the dragons and the people in Betwixt ... and eventually replaced Quarg as king."

"The first Dragonhearth!" Edvard nodded in appreciation. "So did Vronk finally get his name?"

"You mean for fulfilling his Naming Quest?" the old man stirred the fire slightly with the poker iron.

"Yes!" Edvard huffed. "Did he get his dragon name?"

"Why, yes he did," the old man said, looking up from the fire and into the bard's eyes. "And, in fact, my dear Edvard, that is my true gift to you this Yuletide Eve."

"I thought the story was the gift," Edvard shrugged.

"It is," the large man said as he straightened up and stretched. "I know your calling, Dragonsbard, and how voracious that dragon Khrag is for tales. You will, of course, tell this story to the dragon. Any dragon might find this tale amusing but it is Vronk's dragon-name that will make this tale the best gift of all."

Edvard was puzzled. "It is?"

"Vronk's dragon name was Kejathrax," Old Nicholas said with a smile.

Edvard's brow furrowed for a moment as he thought about the name. Suddenly realization came to him and the bard's eyes went wide in wonder. He sputtered as he spoke. "Kejathrax? The great dragon Thrax?"

"That is correct," Old Nicholas laughed. "The father of your very same Khrag. You tell Khrag this tale about his father, friend Bard, and he'll forgive you a year's worth of stories."

The Dragonsbard was, gratefully, speechless with gratitude. It was the finest Yuletide gift he had received in many a decade ... the chance to relax.

"And the reindeer," the Bard asked. "Did they ever learn how to fly?"

"That is a story for another time." The large man pulled back on his coat and his gloves, his great boots strangely silent as he strode across the floorboards of the Inn. He closed the toggles on his coat and adjusted his hat. As he reached for the door latch, he turned toward the Scribe who was dutifully taking everything down.

"Master Abel, I know you, too," smiled the ancient man with the great white beard. "That broach that I gave you. It was not for you to receive; it was for you to give! I have it on the best authority that a rather lovely young woman by the name of Melodi Morgan arrived unexpectedly this very evening at her father's home. If that broach does not suit you, perhaps you might consider giving it to her instead. I should think around nine tomorrow morning would be a good time to call. Ah, but I see that at least one more gift is in order."

With that, Nicholas handed to Abel a bundle of thyme.

"Courage, Abel, comes in many forms," Nicholas said as he pulled open the door. "And a merry Yuletide to all."

The End

Nicholas Fruitcake

(or 'Dragonbites')

Mini-loaf pans make the ideal-size fruitcake. They are perfect for gifting to your favorite dragon.

Ingredients

Dry ingredients:

2 1/2 cups	Goody Mix *(see page 133 below)*
1 tsp.	cinnamon
1/2 tsp.	nutmeg

Fruit and nut mixture:

1 1/2 cups	candied fruit mix
3/4 cup	white raisins
3/4 cup	raisins
1 1/3 cups	candied cherries (red and green)
3/4 cup	dates, chopped
1/2 cup	slivered almonds
1/2 cup	pecan halves

1/4 cup	candied pineapple, coarsely chopped

Wet ingredients:

2 T.	molasses
1 1/2 tsp.	rum flavoring
2	eggs
1/2 cup	orange juice
6 T.	butter, melted (not hot)

Toppings:

Extra nuts and cherries to decorate tops, optional.

After baking:

2 T.	orange juice (brush cakes after cooling)

Directions:

- Preheat oven to 300 degrees.
- Prepare 8 small mini-loaf pans (about 4" x 2"), spraying with vegetable spray and lining with parchment triangles that allow the tips to stick up out of the pan. (This will aid in removing the cakes after baking.)Spray parchment triangles lightly with vegetable spray.
- In a large mixing bowl, stir together the Goody Mix, cinnamon and nutmeg.
- Add the candied fruit mix, all the raisins, candied cherries, dates, almonds and pecans.

- Stir until all fruits and nuts are coated with dry mixture. (This will allow a more even distribution in the batter.)
- In a small bowl combine the wet ingredients; molasses, rum flavoring, eggs, 1/2 cup orange juice and butter.
- Stir till well combined.
- Pour over the fruit and nut mixture and stir with a mixing spoon until all ingredients are wet and evenly coated with batter. (The batter will thinly coat the fruits and nuts.)
- Divide the fruitcake batter evenly between the eight pans.
- Decorate tops of cakes with cherries and nuts as desired.
- Place the eight pans on a large cookie sheet and place in oven.
- Bake 48-52 minutes, turning halfway through baking time and continue baking till cakes springs back when center is touched.
- Allow to cool 15 minutes and gently loosen cake from pans by tugging on parchment edges. If they don't loosen wait until cooled and run a knife around edge of cakes.
- Allow cakes to rest and cool completely before removing from pan.
- Remove from pan and gently peel parchment off of each cake.

- Brush each cake very lightly with orange juice and wrap in plastic wrap and foil.
- Allow cakes to sit at room temperature for up to 48 hours to mellow and then serve or freeze for later use.

Baker's Secrets:
- If cake is chilled before slicing it is easier to make perfect, thin slices of fruitcake.
- For freezing, double bag loaves in freezer-strength plastic bags. May remain frozen up to 6 months.
- Yields 8 mini-loaves.

Recipe for the Goody Mix can be found at
http://bakingoutsidethebox.com

Learn more about Dragonsbard at:
http://dragonsbard.com

Discover how you can write and publish novels just like this one at:
http://scribesforge.com

Learn more about the authors at:
http://trhickman.com

NYT Best-selling fantasy authors Tracy Hickman, with his wife Laura, began their journey across the 'Sea of Possibilities' as the creators of 'Dragonlance' and their voyage continues into new areas with the release of Tracy's 'Drakis' trilogy and 'Wayne of Gotham', a Batman novel for DC Comics. Tracy has over fifty books currently in print in most languages around the world. A record of both Tracy and Laura's DNA currently orbits on the international space station and he is the writer and editor of the first science-fiction movie actually filled in space.

Made in the USA
Charleston, SC
15 December 2012